"We Need To Talk," Tom Rasmussin Said.

Jacy James walked toward him. His gaze slid to her belly. It looked flat still. He had a sudden, visceral memory of her. Oh, yes, he did want her, wanted to touch her one more time, wanted the thrill and insanity of losing himself in her. He'd never experienced fire like hers before that night, their one night together.

She damned sure didn't look like a mother-to-be. But she was carrying *his* baby.

He took a ragged breath, fighting back the welling emotion. "I want to do the right thing, Jacy."

"Good. That's good." She even smiled.

"You want to also, don't you?"

"Of course." The smile tilted into a frown.

"All right, then, will you marry me?"

Dear Reader,

Where do you read Silhouette Desire? Sitting in your favorite chair? How about standing in line at the market or swinging in the sunporch hammock? Or do you hold out the entire day, waiting for all your distractions to dissolve around you, only to open a Desire novel once you're in a relaxing bath or resting against your softest pillow...? Wherever you indulge in Silhouette Desire, we know you do so with anticipation, and that's why we bring you the absolute best in romance fiction.

This month, look forward to talented Jennifer Greene's *A Baby in His In-Box,* where a sexy tutor gives March's MAN OF THE MONTH private lessons on sudden fatherhood. And in the second adorable tale of Elizabeth Bevarly's BLAME IT ON BOB series, *Beauty and the Brain,* a lady discovers she's still starry-eyed over her secret high school crush. Next, Susan Crosby takes readers on The Great Wife Search in *Bride Candidate #9.*

And don't miss a single kiss delivered by these delectable men: a roguish rancher in Amy J. Fetzer's *The Unlikely Bodyguard;* the strong, silent corporate hunk in the latest book in the RIGHT BRIDE, WRONG GROOM series, *Switched at the Altar,* by Metsy Hingle; and Eileen Wilks's mouthwatering honorable Texas hero in *Just a Little Bit Pregnant.*

So, no matter *where* you read, I know *what* you'll be reading— all six of March's irresistible Silhouette Desire love stories!

Regards,

Melissa Senate

Melissa Senate
Senior Editor
Silhouette Desire

Please address questions and book requests to:
Silhouette Reader Service
U.S.: 3010 Walden Ave., P.O. Box 1325, Buffalo, NY 14269
Canadian: P.O. Box 609, Fort Erie, Ont. L2A 5X3

EILEEN WILKS
JUST A LITTLE
BIT PREGNANT

SILHOUETTE *Desire*
Published by Silhouette Books
America's Publisher of Contemporary Romance

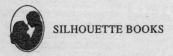

SILHOUETTE BOOKS

RECYCLED PAPER

ISBN 0-373-76134-1

JUST A LITTLE BIT PREGNANT

This edition published by arrangement with Harlequin Books S.A.

® and TM are trademarks of Harlequin Books S.A., used under license. Trademarks indicated with ® are registered in the United States Patent and Trademark Office, the Canadian Trade Marks Office and in other countries.

Printed in U.S.A.

Books by Eileen Wilks

Silhouette Desire

The Loner and the Lady #1008
The Wrong Wife #1065
Cowboys Do It Best #1109
Just a Little Bit Pregnant #1134

EILEEN WILKS

is a fifth-generation Texan. Her great-great-grandmother came to Texas in a covered wagon shortly after the end of the Civil War—excuse us, the War Between the States. But she's not a full-blooded Texan. Right after another war, her Texan father fell for a Yankee woman. This obviously mismatched pair proceeded to travel to nine cities in three countries in the first twenty years of their marriage, raising two kids and innumerable dogs and cats along the way. For the next twenty years they stayed put, back home in Texas again—and still together.

Eileen figures her professional career matches her nomadic upbringing, since she tried everything from drafting to a brief stint as a ranch hand—raising two children and any number of cats and dogs along the way. Not until she started writing did she "stay put," because that's when she knew she'd come home. Readers can write to Eileen at P.O. Box 4612, Midland, TX 79704-4612.

This book is for my friend Gayle,
whose support has meant so much to me.
It's also for the people of Houston,
a wonderful, sprawling megalopolis of a city
as vital as it is varied.
I hope they will overlook the small liberties
I've taken with my fictional version of their city.

One

The woman sitting across from Dr. Nordstrom didn't fit in his pleasant pastel office.

He'd redecorated after buying the practice last winter. Studies had shown that patients found white cold and clinical, so the decorator had used pale peach for the walls, with muted blues and greens for the carpet and accents— colors intended to soothe anxious patients.

Dr. Nordstrom doubted that Jacinta Caitlin James's presence had ever soothed anyone. Particularly anyone male.

She was too vivid, for one thing, in her crimson top and her gauzy skirt splashed with tropical flowers. She was too exotic, with her Gypsy's hair, her tip-tilted eyes and full breasts.

She was also suddenly too pale. Much too pale.

"Ms. James?" he said. "Ms. James, are you all right?"

Jacy's name echoed hollowly in her ears, as if the doctor were calling her from the other end of a long tunnel. "I'm fine," she said automatically. In defiance of the darkness lapping at the edges of her vision, she pushed to her feet.

"Please sit down, put your head between—"

"I'm fine," she repeated as she waited for the dizziness to pass.

Over the years Jacy had been called a lot of things, from persistent to pigheaded. Any number of cops, crooks and politicians had referred to her as "that damned reporter," but even her detractors agreed she was as compulsively truthful in print as she was passionate about lost causes and underdogs. Her co-workers at the *Houston Sentinel* had nicknamed her "Outlaw" in honor of her comfortable relationship with chaos, and her boss had once, in a fit of good humor, been heard to call her the best investigative journalist in the state.

The one name Jacy had never expected would apply to her was *Mother*.

She inhaled raggedly. The darkness receded, leaving her standing in the middle of Dr. Nordstrom's pleasant office. He sat behind his big desk looking up at her with an expression of professional concern. The way the oval lenses of his glasses reflected the overhead lights made them seem to be winking at her.

He had no wrinkles. That bothered her. How could he know enough to advise her on what was happening with her body when his face was as smooth as a baby's behind? Jacy didn't want to look at his too-smooth face. She didn't want him looking at her. Quickly she glanced around the office as if she might find an escape route.

A picture on the nearest wall caught her attention, and she took four quick steps to it. Her skirt swirled around her legs, and if the rest of the world swirled a bit, too, she was convinced she could ignore it.

The picture was an artist's rendering of a woman's torso featuring the poor lady's insides. Her exposed womb held a baby curled up, head down. Both the baby and the woman had pinkish pale skin.

Jacy didn't. People often assumed she was part Mexican, and maybe she was. She didn't know. Her dusky complexion might have been due to a number of possible heritages, from Mediterranean to Bedouin—but her eyes, those Irish green eyes, announced some international mixing and mingling in her genetic past.

"So when am I due?" Her voice was steady, which pleased her. Her question even made sense. Maybe her brain *was* working, even if her head felt stuffed with ghosts instead of thoughts—haunted, irrational wisps she couldn't quite grasp.

"Next March."

"Of course." Apparently her brain wasn't working after all. It hadn't occurred to her to add nine months to the only possible date of conception.

Conception? A hint of wonder slipped past the other emotions. Her hand went to her middle. Her palm felt warm on her midriff through the stretchy knit of the top she'd chosen that morning because the bright red reminded her of courage, and of Sister Mary Elizabeth.

"Ms. James, this has obviously upset you. Please, sit down."

"I'm fine," she repeated. "I just...don't know how to do this." Now there was the understatement of the decade. How could someone who'd never had parents *be* one? She shook her head.

More gently, he said, "You must have suspected your condition when you made the appointment to see me."

But she hadn't *believed* it. That was one of the reasons she'd given herself for not mentioning the possibility to Sister Mary Elizabeth on her visit last Saturday. "Look," she said, turning around, "I'm no more logical than most people. I guess I knew...but it didn't seem possible. I haven't been sick in the morning or anything. And..."

And it had been just that one night, she wanted to cry. It wasn't fair, not fair at all—and if that plaintive thought made her feel closer to sixteen than thirty-one, well, wasn't an unplanned pregnancy something that happened to careless teenagers? Not to a savvy career woman who respected herself too much for casual sex—who had never even been tempted to have a one-night stand. Never, until that night two months ago.

Not that she'd known it was going to be a one-night stand. Not even when Tom had climbed out of her bed and started pulling his clothes on. Not until he'd paused on his way out the door and looked at her. ''This was a mistake,'' he'd told her. Then he'd walked out.

Jacy held her head high and firmed her shoulders. ''He used protection.''

''Yes, and condoms are quite reliable when used with a spermicide, but I believe you said you didn't use any cream or foam.'' Dr. Nordstrom shook his pale blond head. ''The sheath was probably torn or improperly applied. People accustomed to other methods of birth control sometimes find condoms a bit tricky to put on.''

She smiled without humor. Somehow she didn't think Tom lacked experience in donning protection. But he had been in a hurry, hadn't he? Oh, yes, he'd been urgent enough. She'd thought him as desperate, as involved, as she was.

Memories pushed at her from where she kept them trapped deep inside—dark, heated memories that she fought back down. She never wanted to feel again what she'd felt that night.

When she shook her head to chase the ghosts away she realized the smooth-faced doctor was speaking.

''...need to know, first, whether you intend to continue with this pregnancy.''

''Continue—oh, God.'' Abruptly she did want to sit down. She came back to the pale green chair that faced the doctor, and sat. She hadn't thought...hadn't even considered...

As quickly as spring in Houston turned into the baked heat of summer, Jacy turned an inner corner. In that instant what the doctor had told her became true and real. "Yes," she said. Her hand went to her still-flat stomach. "I want my baby." A baby. *Her* baby. However many doubts and fears threatened her, she had no doubts at all about keeping her baby. That certainty steadied her.

"Very well. I'm afraid my predecessor's records are not complete, so I must ask you a few questions. Your medical history doesn't identify your ethnic background."

"Pick one." She gestured widely. Her old doctor had known about her, and briefly she resented the stranger who'd taken his place when he retired last year. "I was raised in an orphanage. I have no idea who my parents were."

"I see." He frowned, tapping the medical record on his desk. "Also, the nurse said you refused to discuss the father's identity. We are not being nosy, Ms. James. For the sake of your baby's health as well as your own, I need medical information on the father, particularly since you have Rh-negative blood."

She was going to have to tell Tom.

For one brief, craven moment Jacy reached for a way, a trick, some justification for keeping this from him—something other than the fact that the idea of contacting him made her sick to her stomach. But Jacy had spent the past several years of her life fighting to uncover and report on the truth. She was no good at avoiding or concealing it.

God help her, she would have to tell him.

"Ms. James?"

"Give me a few days," she managed. "I'll get his medical history, or have him come in and fill out some of your forms. Just give me a few days."

When she left Dr. Nordstrom's office fifteen minutes

later she had a prescription for vitamins, an appointment in another month and a couple of colorful brochures.

It was August, it was Houston, and it was hot. By the time she crossed the parking lot, sweat dampened the nape of her neck beneath the heavy fall of her hair. She slid into the cherry red '65 Mustang she'd finished having restored last year, leaving the door open to let some of the sunbaked air out. The humidity was high that day, and the car's interior felt like a sauna. The white leather seat burned the back of her legs through the crinkled cotton of her skirt.

Jacy welcomed the heat. It made her feel more real.

She started the car to get the air-conditioning going, and then she just sat there with her door open, listening to the radio. The sound of the Beach Boys praising California girls rolled over her comfortingly.

Jacy loved old rock music, especially the soppy, sentimental songs of the fifties. Few people were aware that she had an equal weakness for old TV shows like "Lassie," "My Friend Flicka" and "Leave It to Beaver."

When Jacy was seven and a half, Sister Mary Elizabeth had moved her to the top bunk in the room she shared with three other girls, right above the newly arrived Seraphina Pfeister. Seraphina's nightmares had lasted for months, long past the time it took for her arm to come out of the cast, her bruises to heal and her mother to start serving her sentence for child abuse.

Jacy used to lie in that upper bunk and plan her marriage to Beaver's big brother, Wally. The lavish wedding. A wedding dress so full-skirted no ordinary human could have walked down the aisle in it. The two-story house they would live in afterward and the pets she and Wally would have.... Oh, yes, that had been a favorite daydream. Even after Sera stopped crying at bedtime, Jacy had liked to lie in bed and think up names for the dogs she and Wally would have.

She had known then that her "plans" were fantasy, just

like the old sitcoms. It hadn't mattered. Those fantasies had nourished something in her.

Jacy sat now in her gradually cooling car and tried to remember if she had ever fantasized about having a baby. A puppy, yes. She'd longed quite hopelessly for a puppy to take care of. But another whole, entire human being? Had she ever thought she could be responsible for anything as helpless and endlessly important as a baby?

When she shivered, it wasn't from any outside chill.

Jacy closed her car door at last and slipped her seat belt into place. She picked up the cellular phone she kept in her car for calling in stories or getting answers while trapped in traffic, and punched in a number she knew by heart.

Tabor answered his own phone for once. She told him she'd be out the rest of the day, doing research.

She would be, too. Jacy only knew one way to approach a problem—head-on. She intended to get a grip on her situation the same way she explored a story on any unfamiliar topic. She'd look up what the experts had written on the subject before she tried to figure her particular angle. There were bound to be plenty of experts on a subject as important as motherhood.

She just regretted the half-truth she'd told her boss. Tabor would have to know about her pregnancy soon, of course. He wasn't just her boss, after all. He was her friend.

But she wouldn't tell him quite yet, she thought as she pushed in the clutch and shifted into Reverse. Another man had to hear the news first. However much the idea turned her stomach, however little consideration he rated otherwise, Tom would have to know he was going to be a father.

Her baby *deserved* a father.

But that, too, would have to wait. Jacy felt lost in the suddenly altered landscape of her life. She was too unsteady to face the man who'd walked out on her. Friday, she decided as she shifted gears and pulled out into traffic.

She'd tell him on Friday, four days from now.

In the meantime, she had some research to do.

Four days later

The carpet on the fourth-floor office of the Houston police headquarters building was gray. So were the battered metal file cabinets lining one wall of one of the offices in the Special Investigations section. Late-afternoon sunlight streaked through the blinds of the office's single window to land in hot bars on the gray carpet, the corner of one file cabinet and the left shoulder of the man who sat at the big metal desk.

It was a broad shoulder, covered in white cotton with thin blue stripes. On that Friday afternoon the desk was full but orderly, with a black Stetson hat placed brim-up on one corner and the usual office paraphernalia neatly arranged. An extension to one side held a computer. The credenza behind the man held nine neat piles of papers and miscellany, and four family photos in brass frames.

Another photograph, larger than the rest, sat on the corner of his desk. Those pictures provided the only color in the office.

Tom Rasmussin seldom chained himself to the desk for the entire day, but he'd arrived before the sun this morning and stayed in the office all day, trying to clear away enough paperwork to go to the family beach cottage at San Padre Island with his brother this weekend.

His early arrival that morning was nothing unusual, though. He normally came in early and left late. There was no one to object to the hours he kept. Not anymore.

He was working on the last report when his office door opened. When he glanced that way, one corner of his mouth turned up. "Aren't they checking IDs downstairs anymore?"

The man who sauntered into Tom's immaculate office wore torn jeans, a three-day beard and a faded black

T-shirt with an obscene suggestion printed in Spanish on the front. A greasy bandanna tied Indian-style across his forehead held shaggy light brown hair out of his eyes. "Hey, you got a problem with how I look, man?" He stopped and glanced up and down his grungy body. "I don't see anything wrong. I even changed my underwear this morning."

Tom leaned back in his chair. "I'm surprised you're wearing any. Maybe you should run by Mom and Dad's place and get her opinion on your wardrobe."

"Think she'd give me hell, don't you?" Tom's only brother grinned, turned one of the wooden chairs around backward and straddled it. "If there's any woman who would understand, it's Mom."

Raz had a point. After being married to a cop for forty-one years, Lydia Rasmussin understood the necessities of police work, including undercover assignments. "Even the shirt?" Tom said, raising both eyebrows.

"Hey," Raz said, "you're conservative enough for both of us. Do you even own any shirts that aren't white?"

Tom grunted. "Run along and get some coffee, why don't you, and quit bothering the grown-ups."

"Are you kidding? That stuff's bad for you." Raz shuddered. "Especially the sludge you desk jockeys in S.I. brew. You aren't ready to go?"

"I'll be done in fifteen minutes, if you can be quiet that long." Tom turned back to his computer.

Raz didn't have a problem with being quiet, but sitting still was another matter. After a moment he stood and moved restlessly around the room. Raz had been known to say that his brother got the family quota of patience while he got all the charm.

Few people took the two men for brothers on first glance, or even on second. Both had their father's bone structure, the sort of angular face Clint Eastwood had made famous a generation earlier, but in other ways they were opposites.

Tom's hair was nearly black. Raz's was light brown. Yet it was Tom who had the pale eyes, while Raz's were cocker spaniel warm. Tom was cool, orderly and reserved; Raz was outgoing, energetic and worried about his brother.

His drifting carried him over to the window. He ran a finger along one of the slats of the blinds. ''This office is revoltingly neat, you know.''

''Send a complaint to maintenance,'' Tom said without looking up, ''so they'll quit doing such a good job.''

The office wasn't just clean, Raz thought. It was sterile. Like everything else in Tom's life since Allison died. He didn't know what it would take to jolt his brother out of the half-dead existence he'd settled into after the initial grief faded.

Dynamite, maybe? Tom was one stubborn son of a bitch. He wandered over to the wall where Tom's various certificates and awards were distributed. ''Got your gear together?''

''It's in the Jeep.''

''Want to check out that new exotic dance club while we're down there?''

Tom grimaced and reached for a small black notebook, checking something in his report against his notes. ''Not much point in getting hot and bothered and then going back to the cottage with you, bro.''

Raz shrugged, unsurprised. It wouldn't occur to Tom that he didn't necessarily have to go back to the cottage with only his brother for company. Tom had changed a lot in the three years since his wife died, but he was an intensely private man. Raz couldn't imagine him bringing a one-night stand to the family beach cottage.

A loud *bzzz* announced an in-house call. Tom reached out one long arm, snagged the receiver, and held it between his chin and shoulder, still typing. ''Yeah?''

Raz couldn't hear what the caller said, but he couldn't miss his brother's reaction. Tom dropped the receiver.

He caught it before it hit the floor, but Raz stopped pacing and stared in disbelief at his normally imperturbable brother.

"What?" Tom barked, then, "No! No, don't send her up. Tell her—uh, tell her I'm about to leave on a trip. I'll call her when I get back." He hung up.

Raz felt a smile starting. "What was that about?"

"Nothing." Tom's expression would have kept anyone but a brother from pursuing the subject.

"Didn't sound like 'nothing' to me." Raz felt downright merry as he straddled the chair once more. "Sounded like you're dodging some woman."

"Don't be any more of an ass than you have to." The phone rang again, and Tom grabbed it. "What?" he barked. In the pause that followed, his expression went from forbidding to deadly. "Send her up," he snarled, and slammed the phone down.

"Fantastic." Raz grinned and thought hopefully of dynamite. "I can hardly wait to meet this woman."

"Get out of here."

"No way. I wouldn't miss this for anything."

Jacy had been to police headquarters before, of course, for press conferences or general badgering purposes. So she was familiar with the security, from the heavy steel door the desk sergeant unlocked electronically, to the visitor's badge she clipped on her shirt, to the cameras perched in every corner like metal-and-glass spiders.

The flutter of panic in her stomach wasn't familiar, but the fury that powered her into the elevator and out again almost drowned out other feelings.

Almost.

She'd never been to Tom's office. She had never, she reminded herself, even been to his apartment. He'd talked his way into hers.

No, she told herself, her fingers tight and sweaty on the

folder she carried. *Be honest.* Talk hadn't had much to do with it.

She'd wanted him. From the first time she interviewed him about a case two years ago, she'd been fascinated, drawn. Jacy wasn't accustomed to feeling shy, but it had taken her months to get up the courage to let him know she was attracted.

He'd been quite killingly polite when he told her he wasn't interested.

In spite of that, they'd evolved a good working relationship—as good as a cop and a reporter ever had, at least. Tom occasionally fed Jacy information both on and off the record. She sometimes passed him facts or rumors. They met for drinks sometimes to exchange information and argue about who owed whom. Over the past year they had become friends, or very nearly.

If Jacy had taken a little too much care with her clothes and makeup for those meetings, she'd told herself it was wounded feminine vanity that made her care how she looked. Tom had always made it clear he considered their meetings strictly business.

Until the last time they got together—on June tenth, two months and four days ago. He'd called that Friday to ask her to meet him for a drink. She'd gone, expecting business as usual, thinking he wanted a name, maybe, or the down-and-dirty gossip on some public figure. They'd met at the usual place, a bar not far from police headquarters.

From the moment their gazes had tangled that night, she'd known he didn't have police work in mind this time. And she'd been thrilled.

Infatuation. Jacy's lip curled in a sneer as she left the elevator and headed down the long hall, following the desk sergeant's directions. She'd been as blindly, stupidly infatuated as any teenage girl who didn't know better. She'd not only wanted the man, she'd admired him for his integrity, his strength. Around him she'd felt…different. Softer. More alive.

Well, he'd cured her of that, hadn't he?

But at least, she thought, when the subject came up someday, she would be able to tell her child that it hadn't been all physical attraction. Not on her part, at least. Her child…

The clutch of panic, cold and clammy, added to her anger. When the nameplate outside the last office on the left announced that she'd reached her destination, she shoved the door open without knocking—and stopped two feet inside the room.

Tom sat behind his desk, his thick mustache framing a scowl that held all the friendly charm of a half-starved timber wolf. His office was stark, orderly, all-business—pretty much what she'd expected. The only color came from the row of framed photographs behind him, and the one on his desk—a large, professional photo of a pretty young woman in a checked dress.

Another time Jacy might have had to acknowledge what she felt when she saw that prominently displayed picture. Not now.

She and Tom weren't alone. Another man, a stranger, grinned at Jacy from where he sat on a wooden chair. He was as dirty, disreputable and smiling as Tom was clean, controlled and angry.

It hurt. It shouldn't have, not anymore. But Tom truly hadn't wanted to see her or speak with her. Not even for these few moments. She'd had to threaten to tell the sergeant downstairs why she'd come before Tom would agree to see her—and he still hadn't bothered to grant her privacy.

Well, so be it. She straightened her shoulders and marched up to his desk.

"I don't care much for your methods," Tom growled. "I don't know what you hoped to accomplish, but—"

"Shut up, Rasmussin." She slapped the folder she'd been clutching on the desk between them. Then, for the first time in two months, she met his eyes.

Oh, God. His eyes...colorless as rain, looking at her...looking right through her. Her stomach jumped, and lower down a knot of feeling tightened and spread electrically. A hateful, detestable feeling. She couldn't crave this man anymore. She *wouldn't*.

"Aren't you going to introduce me, Tom?" the dirty stranger asked, still grinning.

"Shut up, Raz." Tom reached for the folder that held the papers she'd drawn up after some of her research. "What the hell is this?"

Raz? Mr. Law-and-Order had had a brother, she remembered. A brother who worked undercover. She gave the bum in the wooden chair a measuring glance, then turned back to face the neatly groomed bum behind the desk.

Jacy smiled a nasty, satisfied smile. Tom really should have agreed to talk to her privately.

She leaned over his desk and tapped the folder. "This is a summary of my probable medical expenses, with the amount my insurance should cover indicated. I'll expect you to pay for half the remaining balance. That's not negotiable. I've also made some suggestions about support payments and visitation rights. Do take your time to think this over—just as long as you get back to me by Monday. That way you'll save us both some legal fees and court costs...Dad."

His face went as suddenly pale as hers had at the doctor's. Satisfied, she turned around and marched out.

Two

At 10:20 that night Jacy pulled into the parking lot of her apartment. She wore a yellow T-shirt with the sleeves torn out over a hot-pink leotard and turquoise bike shorts. Her windows were down, though the temperature still hovered near eighty. After a workout she liked to feel the wind on her damp skin as she drove home, even if it was only muggy city air lifting her hair from her neck.

Another woman might have called a friend after the confrontation with her baby's father. Although Jacy considered a couple of people at the paper good friends, it didn't occur to her to call them. Not then. Instead, she'd driven for hours, using the excuse of an interview to hit the highway. When that didn't help, she'd gone to her gym to try to work through her emotions physically.

That hadn't done much good, either.

Jacy's neighborhood straddled the line between respectable and scary. Her apartment complex was fifty years old and hadn't been anything special even when new, but it was centrally located and she liked it. The walls were thick, the plumbing worked and every spring the azaleas burst into exuberant bloom.

No flowers bloomed this late in the summer. Tonight the air smelled of exhaust fumes and charcoal from the fast-food place down the street.

Jacy turned off the engine, rolled up her windows, grabbed her tote in one hand and her pepper spray in the other. She'd taken three steps away from her car when she saw the man sitting on the outside steps to her apartment. Waiting. Watching her.

She froze.

Night and the harsh light from the lamppost nearby laid hard black shadows across the man's face and form, turning him into a fluidly changing study in black and white as he stood. His hat threw his face in shadow, but she didn't need to see his features to know whose body uncoiled from one of the lower steps.

"If you have to carry pepper spray to walk from your car to your apartment, you're in the wrong neighborhood," Tom Rasmussin said.

The sudden starkness of Jacy's face hit Tom like a blow to the stomach. He hadn't meant to frighten her. But then, he hadn't intended most of what he'd done to this woman, had he?

Guilt had a bad taste, yet there were worse emotions. "We need to talk," he said.

She walked slowly toward him. Damn, it ought to be illegal for women to wear those exercise clothes in public. Especially a woman like her. Jacy had a body that could make a strong man beg, a body he remembered only too well.

His gaze slid to her belly, mostly hidden now by the yellow T-shirt. It looked flat still.

"You picked a lousy time to talk," she said. "It's late."

"This isn't exactly the time I picked. I've been waiting here two hours."

For the first time she smiled. It wasn't a pleasant expression. "You would have waited longer if I'd known you were here."

He didn't doubt that. "I'd like to come up."

She studied him a moment longer before nodding. He didn't need to be a mind reader to know how reluctant she was to let him in—every stiff muscle of her body as she passed him on the stairs spoke clearly of how little she wanted to be around him. He didn't much blame her. The night probably wouldn't get any better for her, either, considering what he had to say.

Her apartment made him jumpy. The large living area overflowed with color and clutter...and memories of the one other time he'd seen it. Books and magazines were scattered everywhere, from the hedonistic couches crowded with pillows to the small dining table where her computer sat.

The book on top of the nearest pile had a picture of a mother and a baby on the dust jacket. Tom looked away.

She'd told him *no* that night. After a long, hot kiss, she'd told him he was going too fast. His hand had been on her breast. She'd looked up at him with eyes slumberous with hunger and shiny with feelings he should have respected—and he'd never hesitated.

It hadn't been hard to change her mind.

Tom took a deep breath. He'd known this wouldn't be easy, hadn't he? He took off his hat and bent to set it on her coffee table.

"You want a drink?" Jacy asked.

He looked at her, standing stiff and wary at the other end of the red couch. Her hair fell loose around her shoulders as if she'd just climbed out of bed. He had a sudden, visceral memory of her, of how she *felt* from the inside—and he wanted her. Oh, yes, he did want her, wanted to touch her one more time, wanted the thrill and insanity of losing himself in her, letting the fire have them both until everything else, past and future, was burned away. He'd never experienced fire like hers before that night, their one night together.

Memory melted into fantasy. What would it be like if he reached for what he wanted and tumbled her down onto one of the brightly colored couches? What if he slid his hand up under that yellow T-shirt as they fell...

Hell, was he completely crazy? He ran a hand over his hair, shaken by how quickly he lost control. "You shouldn't drink, in your condition."

Her lips tightened. "You have a pretty low opinion of me, don't you?" She turned. "I'm having a diet soda. Join me or not, as you choose."

He watched the sweet sway of her hips in that skintight thing she was wearing and hardened even more. She damned sure didn't look like a mother-to-be. *Jock*, he thought, but didn't say. He'd called Jacy that on more than one occasion, giving her a hard time because she liked to work out—partly because it bugged her, but mostly because it had helped him pretend he didn't see her as a woman.

He forced his eyes to move up, and said the first of the things he'd come there to say. "How sure are you that I'm the father?"

She stopped a few steps away and turned slowly. "What do you mean?"

"I mean that I used protection. Both times. Before I accept responsibility, I want to know why you picked me for the father instead of one of your other lovers."

She moved fast. He would have had to really work at it if he'd wanted to stop her. He didn't.

Her slap rocked his head back. When her arm drew back to repeat the action, he caught her wrist. "I'm sorry," he said as gently as he could while struggling with his own pain—a dull, terrible ache trying to swallow him, an ache that had nothing to do with the way his cheek stung from her blow. "I had to ask."

He couldn't doubt her anymore, as much as he wanted to.

She was carrying his baby. Oh, God, she was carrying his baby. Abruptly he turned away, stalking over to the window, where floor-length drapes closed out the night. He stood with his back to her.

There was no doubt in Tom's mind what he had to do. Twenty years on the force hadn't destroyed his belief in certain absolutes. He would do what was right.

He didn't expect it would be easy, though. Or without cost. "You think I could still have that drink?"

The last thing he expected was her low, ragged laugh. "Sure, why not? Wish I could join you. Scotch, right?"

"Yeah. Thanks." On the times they'd gotten together for a drink to exchange information, Tom had usually had a single shot of scotch, neat. He wasn't surprised that she'd noticed. Jacy was damn good at her job—good enough to be a royal pain at times—and reporters of her caliber paid attention to details.

Of course, he knew what she'd had to drink at every one of their meetings, too—everything from orange juice to diet cola to tequila. Jacy liked to have candy bars or greasy hamburgers for lunch and steamed vegetables for supper. She was the least consistent health nut he knew. He'd told her that, too, in the past. Back when they were friends of sorts.

He took his time turning around, waiting until he had himself back under control. When he did, she was nowhere in sight and a brief, absurd spurt of panic stirred in him.

"I can't find the scotch," she said. Her voice came from beyond the dining alcove, where an open doorway gave him a glimpse of a tiny kitchen. "Is beer okay?"

What had he thought—that she'd left? Gone to the store? Moved out of town? "Whatever you've got is fine."

He started moving around the room, examining it with his own eye for detail. He wanted—needed—to know more about this woman who would be the mother of his child. He'd lusted after her for nearly two years, but he'd been careful not to learn too much about her.

It was an absence, not a presence, he noticed first. There weren't any photographs, either framed or in albums. No family photos, because Jacy didn't have any family.

Emotion welled up inside him like blood from a gut wound, a feeling livid and nameless in its complexity. Guilt was part of it. And fear.

Tom believed in honesty the same way he believed in the rule of law. One was necessary to keep the jackals from taking over; the other was essential to keep a man's soul clear of the unpayable debt of regrets. Yet in that moment he knew he would do whatever he could to keep Jacy from learning the truth about the night he'd taken her to bed.

The knowledge didn't comfort him.

Jacy's tastes in reading were eclectic. She seemed to like everything from Sartre to Garfield the cat. A text on agricultural methods sat on the coffee table next to a ragged Rex Stout paperback and a slim book on aromatherapy…and several volumes on childbirth and parenting.

He took a ragged breath, fighting back the welling emotion.

So. She was bright, and curious about pretty much everything. He'd known that much. She was also messy. In addition to the books and magazines scattered around the living room he saw two pairs of shoes and a shopping bag. The coatrack near the door held an umbrella, a fanny pack, a T-shirt and a towel.

So she didn't spend a lot of time picking up. That might be a problem, he conceded. He preferred order. But he didn't see dirt—no unwashed glasses, empty pizza boxes, crumbs or spill marks on the couches or carpet.

Untidy, but clean. He nodded. He could live with that.

The dining table held a computer, printer, printouts, books, newspapers—everything that a reporter might use in a home office. Her mail sat there, as well, in two piles— one opened, one not. He picked up the unopened pile in- stead of the opened one—his version of respecting her pri- vacy—and was sorting through it when she came out of the kitchen with a glass of pop in one hand, a mug of beer in the other and a scowl on her face.

He wondered if she was going to throw the mug at him.

"What do you think you're doing?" she demanded.

He put her electric bill back in the unopened pile. "The same thing you'd do if you were at my place, I imagine. You and I may not have much in common, but we're both nosy by nature and by profession."

She grimaced and held out his mug.

He couldn't help smiling as he took it. She knew he was right, and as much as she wanted to, she wouldn't deny it. That was one of the things he'd liked about Jacy from the start, one reason he'd fought to overcome his damnable reaction to her to achieve some sort of working relation- ship—she was scrupulously fair.

It was a rare quality. It was also why he couldn't doubt her anymore. If she was certain he was the father, then he was.

He lifted his mug and downed half the beer.

"If you're that eager for oblivion, I'll be glad to hit you over the head with something."

"You already have," he muttered.

"It's obvious you aren't exactly thrilled by my news." Her chin was up, but he saw something in the depths of those jungle green eyes, something very much like fear.

"Hell." He set his beer on a clear spot on the table. "I'm not going to duck out on my responsibilities."

"Are you going to sign the child support agreement I suggested, then?"

"Paying child support won't turn me into a father."

She got that look again, the one that had troubled him earlier, when she saw him waiting for her on the steps—a stark, anemic look, as if something vital had drained out. He hated it.

"No, it won't. And if that's your attitude, well, I'll still take you to court for the money because it's only right. It can go into a college fund. But you can forget about visitation rights."

"That's not what I meant." He ran a hand over his hair. Lord, couldn't he do any of this right? "You aren't going to have to take me to court to get me to support my child."

"You just don't want to be bothered with spending time with the baby, then?" she said, her upper lip lifting in a definite sneer. The expression looked damnably gorgeous on that exotic face. "Don't worry about it. We'll do fine without you."

"No, dammit, listen. I meant that, however much of a shock your news was, I want to be a father to my child. A real father, not a once-a-month baby-sitter."

She didn't give herself away by much…the movement of her throat as she swallowed. The pause that went on a little too long while she collected herself. Another man might not have noticed, or understood that she fought to control emotions swinging in wild, breath-stealing arcs.

Tom noticed.

"Well, good," she said at last. "I'd thought—hoped—you were the sort of man who would want visitation rights, would want…it's important, you know. A child should have a father who *wants* to be a father."

Tom knew Jacy hadn't had a father. Or a mother. "What about you?" he asked quietly. "Are you well? You and…the baby?"

"Sure." She shrugged. "The doctor didn't mention any problems, anyway. I feel fine."

Yeah, she was just fine. Pregnant and alone and scared—though she would deny it. He had a feeling he could have found her in a dead faint and she would deny feeling anything as vulnerable as fear.

"Look," she said, "if I give you the name of my doctor, will you go by and fill out his forms?"

"I want to do the right thing, Jacy."

"Good. That's good." She even smiled—not an entirely successful effort, but she was trying. "With both of us wanting what's best for the baby, we can work things out."

"You do want to do the right thing, too, don't you?"

"Of course." The smile tilted into a frown quickly enough.

"All right, then." He took a deep breath and got it said. "Will you marry me?"

She just looked at him, as expressionless as if he'd spoken in another language. In spite of every reason he had not to, he couldn't keep from smiling at her blank expression. "Marriage," he said. "You *have* heard of it?"

"You're crazy," she said.

"That's not quite the response I'm looking for."

Jacy stared at Tom. She had trouble believing she'd heard what she'd heard. "It's all you're getting." *Nuts,* she thought. *The man is obviously nuts.*

All at once she needed to move. There was nowhere to go, no place to be except here, dealing with this—with *him*—but she didn't have to stand still to do it. "What century are you living in, anyway?" She tossed the words over her shoulder as she paced. "People don't get married because they have to anymore."

"We both want what's best for our baby. Having two parents is best."

"Not if they can't stand each other." Jacy paced as if she were race-walking. When she reached the other end of the room she flung herself into a quick turn.

"I'm not surprised if you can't stand me, under the circumstances. But I don't feel the same."

She scowled at him in disbelief and paused. "So maybe

you don't absolutely detest me. You don't think much of me, period.''

''I...respect you.''

For some reason that infuriated her. ''Don't choke on it!''

''Jacy, I know you don't want anything to do with me. But we're not talking about what you want, or what I want.'' There was something deliberate about his smile, something wicked—oh, yes, definitely wicked—a sexy twitch of his mustache, a knowing gleam in his eyes. ''Though the fact that you want me almost as much as I want you ought to help us make a marriage work.''

She laughed at him. Put her hands on her hips, and laughed. ''Oh, tell me another one. You want me? Sure— you took me out, took me to bed and decided once was enough. If I hadn't gotten pregnant I'd never have seen or heard from you again unless I was interviewing you for the paper.''

''I can't believe a woman like you could be so wrong about this sort of thing.'' He started toward her.

What did he mean by that—''a woman like you''? A woman who had so many lovers she might not be sure which of them fathered her child? Jacy held herself steady against the fresh hurt. ''Look,'' she said, ''I think this discussion is getting out of hand. I am not marrying you or anyone else.''

''Fine,'' he said as he reached her. ''We won't talk for a while.''

Jacy was slow to understand. Later she would try to figure out why she'd been so slow, but now—now all she could do was step back. Only somehow she didn't move fast enough. Or far enough. Even as she moved away he followed, reaching out.

His big hands cupped her face.

She should have been able to move then. He held her face firmly, his wolf-silver eyes fixed on hers—but she wasn't hypnotized. She should have been able to move while he bent slowly over her.

Jacy braced herself. She knew what to expect. The memory of how much Tom Rasmussin demanded of a woman made her body soften and ache for him even as she closed her mind and heart against him.

But he tricked her, damn him.

His mustache was soft. So was his mouth—soft and hot and riveting, gathering all her attention to her own lips as surely as a magnet draws iron. He passed his mouth slowly, gently, over hers. Once. Again…and again. The sweet persuasions of his lips undid her with every pass, unraveling her thoughts and her pride, leaving her balanced in some windless place where nothing existed except the quiet attention his mouth paid hers.

Her lips burned. Her breasts tingled. Her belly ached with the rich lightning pouring into her veins, while a longing as rich and forbidden as moonshine, as clear and potent as moonglow, banished sanity.

She reached for him.

In an instant the past surged up into the present. When her arms slid around him he circled her tightly, pulling her against him—body to body, wrapped tightly in each other's arms, trapped together by passion. His tongue entered her mouth. She tasted him then as she had before, and she went a little crazy.

Jacy's hands insisted on knowing his body again. They raced over him. The ache in her intended to have more than this delirious press of clothed bodies, and her mouth silently told him this was so. In return, Tom kissed her as if he were able to do nothing else, as if his next breath depended on tasting her, knowing her.

Just like he'd kissed her the last time. Before he'd left her without a backward glance.

Jacy didn't cool down as fast as she'd heated up. But her

mind awoke, filled with thoughts as jumbled and unpleasant as the aftermath of a tornado. She wrenched herself away.

Her body was cold, separated from his. In a minute, just a minute, that cold would reach the rest of her, and she'd be able to speak.

"You understand now," he said, his voice hoarse with strain. "I wanted you. All along, I've wanted you."

"And you hated it." She knew it was true even as she spoke—saw the truth of it in the sudden flicker of emotion in his startled eyes. "You wanted me and you hated it." She stepped back another pace, trying to steady herself with distance. And failing. "That's why you never called, isn't it? Because you couldn't stand wanting so much."

"Yes. In part, at least."

She ignored the catch in her breath, the sudden stab of pain, to pursue truth the way she always had. "What's the rest of it, then?"

"Maybe I thought you had feelings for me. Feelings I can't return. Whatever makes a man capable of love died in me, Jacy, three years ago. When I buried my wife."

His honesty was as quick and certain as a sword thrust, and for a second or two she couldn't draw a breath. She answered with equal honesty. "You don't need to worry about my feelings anymore. I thought I felt something for you, too, but I was wrong."

Oh, yes, she'd been wrong. Not about what she'd felt—her feelings had been too strong to mistake, too frightening for her to want to claim them if she hadn't had to. But the man she'd been falling for, the lonely man she'd thought lived inside those pale, watchful eyes, didn't really exist. That's what she'd been wrong about. Because that man, the one she'd always dreamed of finding, was someone a woman could count on, no matter what. That man would never have left her the way Tom had.

"I think," she said, "that you should go now."

She expected him to argue, or even to refuse to leave

until she'd agreed to his stupid proposal. However she might have confused herself about him in some ways, she knew Tom wasn't a man to be turned aside from a course he'd set himself. But he just looked at her. His gaze drifted down her body, and she realized he was looking at her middle, where the baby rested. It gave her an odd, uncomfortable feeling.

He nodded, and bent to pick up his hat from the coffee table, then turned away. At the door he paused, his hat in his hand, and she was reminded of the other time he'd paused on his way out her door.

This time he didn't speak of regrets. "We'll talk more later," he told her. "Be sure to lock the dead bolt behind me,"

The door closed quietly behind him.

Lock the dead bolt? That's all he had to say? Jacy started to laugh, but the high-pitched sound that came out scared her into silence. She stood next to her bright red couch in the living room she'd filled with her things and she wrapped her arms around herself for warmth.

She'd wanted to say *yes*. When Tom asked her to marry him, she'd wanted to say yes. Knowing he didn't love her, couldn't love her, she'd still felt as if she'd come home when he'd put his arms around her. For a few insane minutes she'd wanted to take him on any terms she could have him.

The truth tasted dark and sour, like a bitter candy held too long on the tongue. When she swallowed, it went down like ground glass.

Eventually she moved. Her elbows felt stiff and creaky as she unwrapped her arms from around herself. She walked slowly to the door and slid the dead bolt home just like he'd said, because this world was a very unsafe place indeed, and she had no intention of being taken by surprise again.

Three

Pandemonium was the normal order of things at the *Sentinel* as deadline approached. Saturdays were especially crazy as the paper geared up for the Sunday edition, and this Saturday was no exception. Phones rang. People yelled or cussed. The smell of microwave popcorn competed with that of stale cigarette smoke, though the newsroom was supposedly smoke-free.

A row of glass-fronted cubicles faced the big room where people rushed, typed, argued or talked on the phone. In one of those cubbyholes, the Rolling Stones moaned about a lack of satisfaction from a radio perched high on a cluttered bookcase. Yellow sticky notes bloomed on printouts, clippings and miscellaneous piles of paper that threatened to bury the empty soda cans on the desk. A small ceramic planter held a dead plant surrounded by crumpled candy wrappers.

The nameplate on the desk read simply Outlaw.

No traditional family photos were on display, but two

framed photographs from news stories and three press awards crowded the bit of wall that showed between file cabinets.

Someone down the hall dropped something large and metallic. The resounding clatter drowned out all the other noises, but Jacy didn't notice. Like anyone accustomed to living with a large, noisy family, she was good at tuning the rest out. Surrounded by the clutter of her crowded cubbyhole, she was intent on her story.

The chaos and demands of Jacy's job soothed her. After a miserable night she'd plunged into work that morning the way an Olympic swimmer dives into a pool—with the abandon and discipline of total commitment. She knew who she was here at the paper, what she wanted.

It wasn't a major story. Yesterday a man died of stab wounds. In a city like Houston, death was as commonplace as births, weddings and brutality. But honor required Jacy to treat every article as if it were destined for the front page—no slacking, no skimping.

As soon as she finished the story she sent it, with a few swift keystrokes, to her editor's desk for approval. Her chair creaked as she leaned back in it.

Damn, she was tired. She slipped her sandals off and pulled her legs up onto the chair under the gauzy cover of her loose sundress. Jacy had figured out a couple years ago that an unstructured dress was the coolest thing she could wear in the summer, and she seldom put anything else on from June to the end of September.

She laid her head on her upraised knees for a moment, and sighed. It was close to seven o'clock and she'd been on her feet nearly all day, after getting precious little sleep last night.

"Hey, what are you doing, sleeping on the job?" a cheerful voice asked.

Jacy raised her head. "One of these days," she observed, "that cheeriness is going to get you killed."

Nannette Tompkins grinned and held out a folder. "Records said you wanted this, and I offered to trot it up to you. You have any more of those chocolate-covered raisins?"

Jacy sighed as she took the folder from her friend. Nan was cute. There was no other word for it. She was short and curvy, with frizzy red hair, freckles and a smile to rival the young Sally Field's. "I'm not up for chitchat now, okay?"

"That was obvious from the moment you showed up this morning, growling at everyone. Which is why I offered to bring this file up." She came around to Jacy's side of the desk and opened the bottom drawer. "You talk and I'll listen."

"Go away, Gidget."

"Insults roll off me like water. Oh, here they are." She retrieved what was left of Jacy's stash of chocolate-covered raisins. "Now," she said, sitting in the one extra chair the tiny office boasted, "tell Mama what's wrong. It has something to do with that hunk of a cop you went out with a couple months ago, doesn't it?"

"Nothing's wrong." Since Nan was as shrewd as she was cute, Jacy had little hope of being believed.

Both of Nan's eyebrows went up. "Okay." She tossed a few raisins into her mouth, tilted the chair back and propped her feet on Jacy's desk. "Nothing's wrong. You've just got the world's worst case of PMS and felt like reading some obituaries and it's pure coincidence that the one Records sent you belongs to Rasmussin's wife."

Jacy flushed. "Dammit, Nan, you had no business—"

"I care," Nan interrupted, and for once there was no smile on her round face. "Whether that gives me a right to snoop or not we can argue about later. Now tell me what's up."

Jacy sighed, leaned back in her chair and opened the folder. "I'm pregnant."

Nan's feet came down with a thud. "You're what!"

"You heard me," Jacy muttered. The folder held two sheets of the slick, smeary paper used in the microfilm machine at the morgue, and a glossy photograph. One of the sheets was a copy of an article from a few years ago. The other was an obituary.

"It's his? Rasmussin's?"

"Yeah." Jacy scanned the article. It read:

Three people were killed today when a westbound car crossed the center lane of the Central Expressway and crashed head-on into oncoming traffic.

"Have you told him?"

"Yeah." The article added that the driver of the westbound car had been drinking and was ruled dead at the scene. His victims hadn't been so lucky. One hemorrhaged to death before the ambulance arrived. The other died at the hospital during emergency surgery.

Allison Rasmussin was the one who died in surgery.

"Well? What did he say?"

Jacy took out the photo and tossed the folder on her desk. "He wanted to know why I thought it was his."

Nan used some words that would have gotten Gidget's mouth washed out with soap.

Jacy smiled for the first time. "Look," she said, feeling the strain of the long day settle around her, "I know you mean well, but I need to sort some things out before I talk about it, okay?"

If one of the cubs from the city-hall beat hadn't stuck his head in the door, looking for Nan, Jacy might not have prevailed. But between the rumor of a city councilman's arrest for driving while intoxicated and Jacy's smiling plea for time, Nan was persuaded to leave.

Jacy's smile faded as soon as she was alone again. She looked at the picture in her hand. It was a duplicate of the one on Tom's desk, she realized. Allison Rasmussin still smiled shyly out at the world from it, a delicate Dresden lady in a blue-and-white checked dress.

A pretty woman, Jacy thought—not beautiful, or especially striking. Just pretty. Had she been as delicate as she looked? Had she gone to college, drunk beer, crammed for exams, entered a profession? What had she dreamed, longed for, resented?

Had she loved her husband as much as he still loved her three years after her death?

When Jacy's phone buzzed she dropped the picture on top of the folder, relieved to be dragged away from a subject she kept worrying like a sore tooth. But the interruption wasn't quite the change of subject she'd hoped for.

Her boss was ready to see her now.

Jacy took a deep breath, trying to clear her weary mind. Tabor wasn't going to take the news of her pregnancy well.

Theobold Tabor was over sixty but didn't look it, though the deep grooves along his cheeks suggested his scowl was a frequent fixture. He had long, bony arms and legs, and skin the color of the polished teak cane that leaned against the desk where he sat. Back in the sixties some Klansmen hadn't approved of the series of articles he'd done on civil rights. They'd taken a baseball bat to his knees.

Jacy respected Tabor more than any other journalist on the face of the planet, and she liked him almost as much as she respected him. At the moment, though, she was considering using his cane to hit him over his very hard head. "It's none of your business," she repeated.

"None of my business? You come prancing in here, tell me you need to take maternity leave in a few months and expect me to leave it at that?"

Well, no, she hadn't expected him to "leave it at that." That's why she'd been dreading this discussion. In an office full of professional snoops, Tabor could have won an award, hands down, for being the nosiest. *Especially* with his friends. "My maternity leave is your business," she said. "The name of my baby's father isn't."

Indignation faded into sorrow on Tabor's long face. "I thought we were friends."

"We are, but—"

"You can't trust me?" He put the question quietly. With resignation.

Oh, he was good, all right. Jacy rolled her eyes. "You already gave yourself away when you asked if the 'sorry so-and-so' was going to marry me."

"A perfectly reasonable question."

"I am not going to cater to your medieval ideas by telling you his name. You have no shame. You'd probably call him and tell him he *had* to marry me or something." Jacy shuddered. That was all she needed—having Tabor and Tom both telling her she had to marry for her baby's sake. She'd have to leave the state to get any peace.

"The man should be willing to give his baby a name," he said firmly.

"I've got a name to give my baby. James. I may not know where it came from, but it's a perfectly good name."

He was silent for a moment before switching tacks. "Setting aside my 'medieval' notions, it's not going to be easy raising a child alone. You'll let me know if I can help, won't you?"

"Well," she said, weakly relieved that he'd dropped the cross-examination for now, "I might want to borrow Camille for a few words of advice sometimes." Tabor's wife had raised three children while working full-time as an architect before she and Tabor met and married a few years ago. Jacy figured she'd know plenty about how to balance parenting with a professional life.

"She'll tell you the first thing you need is a supportive husband," Tabor returned promptly. "And I...good God—"

"What is it?" she asked suspiciously.

Tabor grimaced. "Tell me that *isn't* the baby's father coming toward us across the newsroom. Please."

Jacy's whole body jolted. Tom? Here? She turned in her chair—and sighed. The stranger she'd seen in Tom's office yesterday was winding between desks out in the main room. He was dressed slightly better today. His T-shirt was a truly virulent green, but it lacked yesterday's slogan. He still sported the bandanna and a couple days' growth of beard.

"Not the father," she said. "The uncle."

Jacy spoke the words, then stopped. Her baby was going to have an uncle? Her hand dropped to her stomach. She hadn't realized, but...through Tom, her baby would have *relatives*. Like grandparents. An uncle. Maybe some cousins. Everything Jacy had lacked.

She was anxious, suddenly, to know more about Tom's family. What were they like? Would they accept the baby?

"An uncle, eh?" Tabor said thoughtfully.

Jacy grimaced. She'd slipped. Given that much, Tabor would have Tom's identity in a day or two. The man was uncanny that way. "All right," she said, standing. "I'll tell you now if you promise you aren't going to call him and tell him to 'do right' by me."

"You don't really believe I'd interfere in your life that way, calling some man I've never met and—*have* I ever met him?"

"No hints," she said firmly, heading for his door. If she hurried she could intercept Tom's brother before he got here and Tabor interrogated him. "Do you promise?"

"All right, all right. I won't call him."

Which didn't mean he wouldn't go harass Tom in person, but she was out of bargaining time. "Tom Rasmussin," she told him, and turned the door handle.

"The cop?" He sat up straight, astounded. "You're involved with a *cop?*"

"Not anymore," she said, and escaped.

Raz saw Jacy emerge from a glass-enclosed office. As she headed toward him he added details to his impression of her yesterday. Physically she was a knockout, of course—not beautiful, but she fairly shimmered with energy. And her body—*down, boy,* Raz told his own body. He was going to have to learn to think of this woman as a sister.

She asked him to join her in her office. He followed, aware of the half-dozen people staring at them curiously—aware of the sway of her hips beneath her loose, gauzy dress.

He smiled. Maybe seeing her as a sister was asking too much of himself. He could still appreciate the view, couldn't he?

He followed her to a tiny cubicle where the Supremes were singing about being a "love child." She grimaced and switched off the radio. Raz settled in the only chair without waiting for an invitation.

She didn't look happy to see him when she sat behind her desk. She looked wary and tired...and sinfully hot, like a week's worth of mind-blowing sex wrapped up in wrinkled cotton. Hot enough, maybe, to break down the mile-high walls of a certain stubborn fool.

Best of all, she looked nothing at all like Allison. The only other woman who had stirred his brother's interest in the past three years had looked entirely too much like his dead wife. Fortunately, she'd ended up marrying their cousin Seth. "We haven't exactly been introduced," he said with one of his best grins. "I'm Tom's brother Raz, and I am *very* pleased to meet you."

"Raz?" Her eyebrows rose. "I could have sworn it was Ferdinand," she murmured.

He winced. "Apparently my brother's been giving away family secrets."

"Nope. But I'm a reporter. I've got my sources."

He glanced at the folder on her desk, where Allison's photo smiled back at him. "So I see."

She snatched the picture and stuck it back in the folder. "So what can I do for you?"

"First, you can accept my apology. I didn't realize when I insisted on staying in Tom's office yesterday quite how personal your business with him was. I'm sorry I intruded." He hesitated. "Well, I'm sorry if my presence was awkward for you, anyway. I'm not really sorry I was there. This way I got to hear the good news right away."

She hesitated, then smiled tentatively. "I'm glad you consider it good news. Apology accepted."

She was sharp, sexy, successful...and, he realized when he looked at that uncertain smile, vulnerable. Raz recognized that and responded instinctively. He couldn't lust after a woman with wounds hiding in her eyes, wounds he suspected his brother had a lot to do with. "You shook Tom up pretty thoroughly."

"Good."

"He's not really as much of an idiot as he seems, you know. He's...not good with surprises." Raz knew both too much and too little to say more—too much about his brother's side of what had happened between him and this woman, too little about her.

"I don't—" A yawn interrupted whatever else she was going to say.

"Long day?"

"Saturdays always are." She eyed him curiously. "That's the ugliest shirt I've ever seen. You're undercover with Vice, aren't you?"

He laughed. "If you're trying to excuse my taste—"

Her phone rang. She picked it up, shrugging an apology for the interruption. She listened, asked a couple questions, then hung up and stood. "That was my boss," she said, her eyes shiny with excitement in spite of the shadows beneath them. "I've got to go. The old Rutger Hotel is burn-

ing, the reporter who normally covers that beat is on another story and Tabor's holding the front page.''

Big fires are noisy. The sounds of this one reached Jacy
while she was still in her car a couple blocks away—water
roaring and hissing, men shouting and a deep, bass rum-
bling, as if some huge monster were under assault. Adrenaline ate at her lingering exhaustion as she hunted for a
parking place—adrenaline and dread.

Her years as a reporter had never taught her how to approach human disaster with detachment. Even as she parked
her car illegally in an alley, she wondered if anyone burned
in the belly of that beast or crouched in one of the yet
untouched rooms, waiting for rescue or death.

But when she shut her car door behind her, she did her
best to shut away both her dread of what she might discover
at the fire, and the last remnants of her fatigue. She had a
job to do.

It was summer, so it was still light outside when she
approached the barricades. And hot. She felt the heat of the
fire sharply through the thin gauze of her dress as she
hunted up witnesses, and she breathed in air that stank of
burning. Smoke billowed out of the windows of the historic
old hotel, chased upward by a lurid underskirt of orange
flame.

Four fluorescent yellow fire engines hemmed in the
blaze. From eighty-five feet off the ground, two men in the
basket of the snorkel truck directed a thousand gallons of
water a minute on the roof of the nearest building. Below,
firefighters in protective gear aimed the powerful umbilical
lines of their fire hoses at the monster devouring the building.

It took Jacy fifteen minutes to confirm that all of the hotel
guests were believed to have gotten out. Within another
half hour she had some names, a possible cause of the blaze
and interviews with the battalion chief and one of the evac-

uees. The fire wasn't out, but it was under control—and back at the newsroom, Tabor was holding a spot on the front page. Time to leave.

Darkness was slipping over the city when Jacy headed back to her car, where her cellular phone waited. She ran possible lead lines through her head as she walked.

Halfway there, she started to feel dizzy.

Jacy was used to good health. She'd never felt anything like the light-headed, fading sensation that swept over her. She stopped, uncertain. A little scared.

Had she forgotten to eat? Yes, she decided. That was it. That's all that was wrong with her—low blood sugar. She'd skipped supper. Obviously delaying meals was a mistake in her condition. After a brief pause she felt slightly better and started walking again.

Then the first cramp hit.

Wounded animals make for their lairs. When the walls of Tom's apartment started closing in on him that afternoon, he headed for headquarters. The window of Tom's office faced west. He stared out at the dying day as the thickening gray of twilight gave way to the darkness that spread itself over the city, watching as lights winked on in windows. Tom had spent half his lifetime defending the people in the houses behind those winking lights from those who preyed on their fellows.

Protect and Defend.

Twenty years ago, when he'd graduated from the police academy and pinned on his badge for the first time, he'd known so much. A man did, at that age. He'd been certain of what he wanted from life and how to get it. He'd wanted to be a cop like his father, and he'd wanted to settle down with a good woman and raise children.

It hadn't occurred to him, at twenty, to wonder whether he deserved either of those sweetest of life's gifts.

By the time he met the good woman twelve years later,

Houston's streets had knocked most of his certainties out of him. He'd still wanted to marry, but he'd no longer dared to want children.

Allison had, though.

Tom turned away from the window and walked to his desk. Slowly he picked up the photo that had sat on the same corner of that desk for six years—three years before Allison died, and three years, now, after.

It wasn't Allison he'd dreamed about last night.

Tom knew what love was. He'd loved his wife, so he knew it wasn't love he felt for Jacinta James. This hot, urgent craving was too selfish, too physical and too nearly desperate to be that tender emotion. But it wasn't anything as simple and clean as lust, either. Lust by itself wouldn't burden him with guilt this way. Lust would have been eased by taking her to bed, not doubled.

Obsession, maybe.

The name didn't matter. Whatever he felt, he was going to have to deal with it, and he hoped, he prayed, he could get a handle on how to do that quickly. She was carrying his baby. His *baby*. He'd treated her badly and she wanted nothing to do with him, and he couldn't blame her for that. But he couldn't let her continue to hold him at arm's distance, either.

He had to change her mind. Somehow, some way, he had to change her mind about marrying him.

Tom stared at the photo in his hand. He couldn't ask Jacy again to marry him while Allison's picture sat on his desk, could he?

The phone rang. Tom set the photo on his desk, face-down, as he picked the receiver up. "Rasmussin here," he said.

"Tom?" The voice at the other end was so shaky and uncertain that for one jarring second he didn't recognize it. "Tom, there's something wrong. Really wrong. I—I'm cramping and I—"

"Jacy? Where are you?"

"I'm in my car near the Rutger. The hotel. There's a fire and I—I'm bleeding." Her voice broke, and she was crying. Jacy, whom he would have sworn could take a beating without crying, choked her words out between sobs. "I'm afraid I'm losing the baby. I'm scared, Tom. I'm so scared!"

"Stay there. Stay right there in your car and I'll get someone to you." He could do this, he told himself. Hadn't he done this hundreds of times, talked to a victim or a witness, kept his voice steady, detached, so they would stay calm while he did his job? "Stay there," he repeated, and his voice broke. "I'll get you some help, Jacy, I swear it."

Four

The emergency room at Medical Center Hospital smelled like hospitals everywhere. The medicinal stink of disinfectant overlaid the faint, grim mingling of sweat, blood and less pleasant odors. Jacy lay on the examining table in a small white room with gleaming metal fixtures and a punishingly bright light. She wore a hospital gown and a thin sheet. A clear plastic tube led to the back of her right hand, where tape held the needle in place while the IV machine hummed as it pumped fluids into her.

The IV made it a little harder to hold Tom's hand, but she managed.

She'd been holding on to him ever since he shoved his way into the room fifteen minutes after she arrived at the hospital in siren-wailing style, driven there by one of the officers from the fire scene. Tom had arranged that.

Even during the discomfort and embarrassment of the exam, she'd held on to him. He'd refused to leave, too—but she hadn't really given him much choice.

One corner of Jacy's mind marveled at herself. When she fell apart for the first time in her adult life, she'd called Tom. It had been the one thought in her mind by the time she reached her car, bent over from a fierce cramp, feeling the thin, terrifying trickle of blood down her leg—she would call Tom and he'd take care of everything. He might not love her or want her, but she'd known on a bone-deep level she could count on him for this. And she'd been right.

Strangely, lying on a cold examining table, waiting to see if she would hold on to the life inside her or not, Jacy didn't think of Tom as the overwhelming lover who'd planted that life in her. She thought of him as the man she'd come to know over the past two years—a hard man, strong, sometimes inflexible. An honorable man.

And now she couldn't let go of him, but she couldn't talk to him, either. She could barely talk at all. Words were her tools, her livelihood, but they were locked up inside her, shut away tight in some frightened pocket of her soul. She didn't dare open the door to let them out. Who knew what would come out with them?

"You okay?" Tom asked softly.

She searched for words she could use. Safe words. "I haven't been in the hospital since I broke my ankle in college," she said. "Not as a patient. Why do they keep it so cold in here? Stupid to keep it so cold when it must be eighty degrees outside."

"I'll get you another cover," he said, and let go of her hand. It took a conscious effort on her part to release his hand in turn so he could move away. He didn't bother to summon a nurse, but went to one of the cabinets and started looking for another of the thin sheets.

Later she would probably be embarrassed, maybe humiliated, over the way she'd been clinging to him. Later she might feel a lot of things. "I didn't know it mattered this much," she whispered. "I've only known about the baby for a few days. I never thought about being a mother, never planned on it. Why does it matter so much?''

He was back, laying a doubled-up sheet over her. Hands she remembered as big and hard and passionately demanding were careful, gentle, as they tucked the sheet over her. A feeling like grief twisted inside her.

''When I was thirteen,'' he said as his hands stilled, resting on either side of her, ''my folks gave me a CB radio for Christmas. I hadn't asked for one, and when I first opened the box I wasn't sure what to think. But by that afternoon I was crazy about that radio. It was a great gift, even if I hadn't known I would want it.''

His eyes met hers—eyes as clear and bleak as rain in December, storm-racked eyes. ''I guess that's a stupid story, comparing a radio and a baby.''

''No.'' The tape pulled on the back of her hand as she reached for his hand again. His fingers closed around hers quickly. *He needs this, too,* she realized with a little jolt that reached past the fear and confusion. *Tom needs this contact as much as I do.*

He wanted the baby, really wanted it, and he was frightened and hurting, just like her.

The knowledge steadied her. She tightened her grip. ''No, it isn't a stupid story. I guess…we don't always know what we need.'' She hesitated, then said, to give him hope, ''I haven't had any cramps for a while now.''

He looked away. ''Well, that's good.'' He studied the wall as if he were talking to it instead of her, but his hand tightened convulsively. ''That's got to be a good sign.''

She'd practically stopped bleeding, too, since reaching the hospital—only a bit of spotting. That was enough to make her hope, but, curiously, hope was almost as hard to endure as waiting. She knew very well that any bleeding at this stage was bad. ''They should be back in soon to tell us about the tests.''

He didn't answer. His face gave nothing away. If she

hadn't been watching closely, she wouldn't have noticed the way his throat worked. "Tom?"

"It's my fault," he said, then burst out, "My God, I don't know why you even want me here. Why you let me be here. I left you alone. You shouldn't have been alone."

She blinked, confused. What did he mean? She shouldn't have been alone tonight, at the fire? She shouldn't have been alone the past two months?

Before she could find words or reasons, the door to their little prison opened, and the doctor who had examined her stepped in. She wore pale blue slacks with the inevitable stethoscope snaked into the pocket of her white lab coat. Short hair framed her round face in a halo of white curls. "Mr. and Mrs. James?"

"I'm Lieutenant Rasmussin," Tom said without moving away from Jacy's side. "Ms. James and I aren't married."

"I see." Quick blue eyes assessed them both. "Are you living together? Normally that would be none of my business, but whether or not I release Ms. James will depend on the amount of care available to her at home."

"I'll take care of her," Tom said.

At the same moment Jacy exclaimed, "Release me? I can go home, then? I—the baby—" She stopped to blink back tears.

The doctor smiled at her. "As far as I can tell, your baby is just fine."

Jacy closed her eyes, dizzy with relief and a huge, enveloping joy. Her baby was all right. "I can go home," she said, to make it real. "But..." She opened her eyes and faced the other half of the truth. "I shouldn't have cramped and bled like that. Something is wrong, isn't it?"

The doctor came closer. "My diagnosis will need to be confirmed, and you'll want to check with your own gynecologist. But my preliminary exam indicates a thinning of the cervix. Tell me, Ms. James, did your mother mention any difficulties in carrying you to term? Something she might have taken medication for?"

"I didn't know my mother."

"I see. Well, it's likely that a drug she took during pregnancy is the cause of your condition. DES was widely prescribed thirty-one years ago to help women in danger of certain types of miscarriage carry babies to term. Unfortunately, the drug caused certain abnormalities in some of those babies, including a thinning of the cervix in the females."

"My mother..." The words, so seldom spoken, felt odd in Jacy's mouth. She glanced from the doctor to Tom and back, bewildered. "No, I doubt she took anything like that. My mother left me at the door of an orphanage. In a basket," she added, striving for the usual wry humor with which she told this story. "With a note pinned to the blanket. She gave me a two-month test run before deciding she'd gotten the wrong model, or just couldn't afford the upkeep." Jacy had come to terms with her abandonment years and years ago. This doctor had no business implying her mother had actually wanted her. She knew differently.

"Yet it looks like she went to some trouble to give birth to you," the doctor said. "But the point now is the effect this has on your own pregnancy. If you want to carry your baby to term, you're going to have to make some major adjustments in your life. First, you'll need to take medical leave from your job."

Jacy couldn't take it in. She tried, but she couldn't make sense of what the doctor said, either about the woman who had borne her, or about her job. She couldn't quit work. That made no sense. Her job was her home, her identity. Who would she be if she weren't at the paper every day?

But she couldn't keep her job, either. That became clear as Tom asked questions and the doctor answered. Gravity had become Jacy's enemy. She was going to have to stay off her feet almost completely for the next week, and to some extent for the duration of the pregnancy.

She would lose her baby if she kept working.

Everything after that was a little blurry. At one point Tom left to speak to the people in the waiting room—people Jacy hadn't known were there. Maybe he'd told her and it hadn't penetrated. His brother was there, waiting to hear about the baby. So was Tabor and Nan and another cop who worked with Tom.

Jacy got dressed while Tom was gone. She was just stepping into her sandals when the doctor stopped in to give her the results of the last blood test.

"Everything looks good. Try not to worry too much," the woman said, patting Jacy's hand. "Some women with a fragile cervix must resort to surgery, but your condition isn't that extreme. Your body stopped bleeding and cramping on its own, which is an encouraging sign. In fact, I'm surprised you had this much trouble this early in the pregnancy. Perhaps you've been under extra stress lately? Or were on your feet an especially long time today?"

"Yes," Jacy said, clenching her teeth against the guilt. "Yes to both. It's my fault, then."

"Your activities helped bring on the bleeding," the doctor agreed bluntly, "but you had no way of knowing that would happen. And it's better to discover this now instead of later." She gave Jacy's hand a last pat. "Go home with your young man now, and let him pamper you. It will make you both feel better."

Jacy looked up. Her "young man" stood just inside the door, waiting with the alert patience that made him a good police officer. She hadn't noticed him come in. But a lot of things were happening that her mind didn't seem to record properly. For example, at some point she must have agreed that Tom was going home with her tonight. She didn't remember doing that, but it was happening, so she must have.

"Ready?" he asked softly.

She nodded. It occurred to her then that something was missing—Tom's hat. He always wore that hat, yet he'd left his apartment without it after she called.

The thought moved her to an absurd degree.

They wouldn't let her walk out. Tom went to bring his Jeep up to the door when the nurse showed up with the wheelchair. Jacy gritted her teeth and made herself joke with Tabor about it, because he was still there, limping alongside her as the nurse wheeled her out.

"You'd better go home," she told him, feeling awkward and out of context as she sat in the wheelchair near the door, waiting for Tom's Jeep to pull up. "I get to sleep in late tomorrow. You don't."

"Editors don't sleep," he said. "Like vampires, we're at our best at night."

It was an old joke, but she smiled anyway.

"Jacy, I would never—I shouldn't have sent you to that fire. I wasn't thinking. You'd just told me about being pregnant, and I wasn't thinking. I should have—"

"No," she said, "there wasn't a thing you should have done differently. You didn't know it would be a problem." He looked worried still. Reacting to a rare impulse, she reached out and touched his arm. "I'm okay, Tabor."

He studied her face closely for a moment. "Yes, I do believe you are, though you may not realize it yourself yet." Tom's Jeep pulled up then, dusty and black, invisible in the night except for the glare of its headlights. Tabor glanced at it and smiled. "I'll stop by tomorrow and we can talk about insurance and such. You've chosen well for yourself, Jacy."

With those ambiguous words he left. Jacy waited for Tom to get out, feeling helpless, a stranger in her own body, dependent on a man who'd left her—and for now, just for tonight, she discovered, she was too tired to care.

She was asleep before they were halfway home.

* * *

Tom laid the sleeping woman carefully in the bed he'd turned down before carrying her up the stairs to her apartment. She hardly stirred. Light from the living room spilled in through the open door, just enough light to show the sweet, lush curves of her body, the sleeping serenity of her face.

Tom sat beside her for a moment, telling himself he was catching his breath. Toting a woman up a flight of stairs wasn't all that easy at forty. Especially at the end of a night like this one.

God, he thought, and it was more prayer than profanity, a mingled plea and thanksgiving. What a night it had been.

His hands shook as he slipped her sandals off. The tremor had nothing to do with muscular fatigue, and everything to do with all he had nearly lost that night. He considered undressing her and decided to settle for unfastening her bra, which he did, then stood. His lower back twinged.

Jacy was no lightweight, that was sure. One corner of his mouth turned up at the thought as he pulled the covers up. She sighed, snuggled into the pillow, and sank more deeply into the sleep her body needed so badly.

No, she was no lightweight. Jacy was strong inside and out, as stubbornly independent as a cat. And even less likely to forgive.

His slight smile faded into grimness. He left her sleeping there, left the bedroom door open behind him as he took care of putting the rest of the place to bed for what remained of the night. He locked the front door and checked the windows before turning off the lamp and sitting on one of her couches. Heaving a sigh, he pulled off his boots. For a moment he sat there in the darkness and let his shoulders slump beneath the weight of guilt and silence.

She had a great deal to forgive. More than she knew. More than he intended for her ever to know. But, he thought as he reached for the afghan that, in the darkness, showed none of its multicolored brightness, he'd take things one sin at a time.

He stretched out on the longest of her two couches and closed his eyes. Best to concentrate on the lie he intended to tell her tomorrow, he decided. Eventually she was going to figure that one out, but with any luck, by then it would be too late.

When Jacy opened her eyes, the sun wasn't peeking through the drapes at her window with its usual early-morning hesitation. Instead it poured through the slit to slap the carpet with the bright, hot glare of midday.

She turned her head and stared at the clock on her dresser in disbelief. Noon? It was twelve o'clock noon?

It wasn't until she sat up in a late-for-work panic that the events of the night before rushed back to her. She clutched her stomach, waiting to feel...something. A cramp, a clue, some evidence of the frightening new fragility of her body. But she felt fine...except that her bra was tangled up beneath her armpits, and she'd slept in her clothes.

Jacy considered that, flushed, and pulled off the dress she'd slept in. Tom must have put her to bed. At least, she thought with an unstable mixture of emotions, he'd done no more than unfasten her bra. She ought to be grateful— he'd tried to make her comfortable without undressing her. He'd done a lot for her last night, and he'd left without embarrassing her this morning.

But whatever she was feeling, it wasn't gratitude.

Jacy threw her bra on the floor and grimaced, remembering the way she'd clung to Tom. She'd been so damned *needy*.

Yet she'd had the impression he'd needed to hold on to her, too. She shook her head, confused by what had been clear and obvious the night before.

Could she have been right? Could Tom really have needed her?

She got up and went to the bathroom, where she took her robe from the hook on the back of the door and considered a shower. Later, she decided. From the way her stomach was growling, food needed to be first on her agenda. After all, she thought as she opened the door of her bedroom, she wasn't going anywhere today, was she?

She was several steps into the living area before the smell of coffee and the sizzle of cooking meat penetrated the muddle of emotions hazing her mind. She frowned...and noticed the Stetson hat placed neatly, brim up, on her coffee table. If Tom's hat was here, so was he.

But Tom wasn't supposed to be here now. It was noon. He should have been long gone, off playing cop.

Then she saw the boxes—two of them, large cardboard boxes like the supermarket throws out every day. The biggest one sat on the floor near the blue couch. It was closed. The flaps on the one next to it were open. She walked over and looked inside, and saw neatly folded piles of clothing.

Men's clothing.

Tom came out of her tiny kitchen. He wore a clean white shirt with the sleeves rolled up and carried her big orange coffee mug, the one with the quote from Mae West that read, *Between two evils, I always pick the one I've never tried before.* "I don't know whether you want breakfast or lunch," he said, "but either way I figure you'll want a cup of coffee first."

She inhaled longingly, lusting after the coffee he was tempting her with. "I'm not supposed to have caffeine."

"It's decaf."

He was being too good to her, too careful of her, too...present. "What are you doing still here?" she burst out.

He raised one dark brow. "Don't you remember? I told you I would take care of you, and you agreed."

"I don't need to be taken care of! And even if I did, you wouldn't need those—'' she gestured wildly at the packing boxes "—to do it.''

"How can I take care of you if I'm not here?'' he asked with infuriating patience. "Of course, we have a lot to settle about what I should bring over and how much time I should take off. You were too groggy last night for us to discuss it in any detail, so I just brought some clothes over for now.''

"You're crazy,'' she said flatly.

"We'll talk after you eat.'' He came farther into the room, and set the mug on the coffee table by the red couch. "What's it going to be—breakfast or lunch? I found hamburger meat in your freezer and tortillas in the refrigerator. I'm cooking the meat with onions and peppers for burritos, if you want lunch.''

She shook her head, not so much at the question as to try to get her brain working. "Why are you here *now?* You can't just call in and take a day off. You're a detective, not a lawyer or a banker or something.''

He smiled. "It's Sunday. Even police detectives get a Sunday off now and again.''

Oh. She'd forgotten. Last night had seemed to drag on for several days.

"We need to decide how much time I should take off this next week.''

That was easy to figure out. "None.''

He didn't seem to be listening. "I won't claim that it's easy for me to take off,'' he said, "but I'm entitled to personal leave for a family emergency.''

A family emergency. He was referring to the baby, of course—but it felt strange, very strange, to be so nearly part of someone's family. Kind of scary. She licked her lips nervously. "I didn't agree to you moving in.''

"You really don't remember, do you? Here, you'd better sit down if we're going to talk about it now.''

"I didn't—"

"You're supposed to stay off your feet, remember?"

Reluctantly she sat within grabbing distance of the coffee steaming gently in its mug. Her afghan, she noticed, had been folded neatly and laid across the back of the couch instead of being tossed over it every which way. "You slept out here last night." She didn't realize until she spoke that she'd been worried he might have slept next to her.

But he'd never wanted that, had he? To take her to bed, yes—he'd wanted her passion and her body, but he hadn't slept with her. He hadn't stayed long enough.

"My presence was the condition the doctor set for releasing you from the hospital. You do remember that, don't you?"

"Yes, but that's all I agreed to." If she'd actually agreed to that. It had just sort of happened.

"You don't remember us talking about it on the way home? Jacy, there's no way you can take care of yourself properly this next week if you stay off your feet as much as you're supposed to."

Jacy frowned at him suspiciously. She didn't remember talking with him on the way home. She didn't remember anything after leaving the hospital. Could she, muddled from exhaustion and trauma, have actually agreed to let this man move in with her?

Tom met her gaze steadily, his eyes a cool, opaque gray this morning. He looked stark, crisp and orderly in the chaotic color of her living room—a black-and-white lawman in pressed jeans and a clean white shirt with grizzled, timber wolf hair.

And she wanted him.

Jacy pulled her eyes away, shaken. He made her ache. In spite of everything, he made her ache—to touch, to be touched—surely, oh, surely, she couldn't want more. Not *now*.

Yet she knew what he smelled like when her face was

pressed into the crook between his neck and his shoulder, knew the way his muscles quivered when she licked him there. And it was too much, simply too much, her desire for this man, the need that bubbled up ceaselessly like the clear, hot water from a hidden spring. Too much, on top of everything else that was topsy-turvy in her life.

For once, Jacy refused to face, straight-out, what had to be faced. "Whatever you're cooking will be okay." Without looking at him she reached for her coffee.

"In that case, lunch will be ready in a few minutes."

"Fine."

Tom studied the woman he was lying to for a moment longer before turning away. He didn't fool himself he'd won, or even that he'd really convinced her. But he was here, and that was enough for now.

Besides, he thought, smiling as he headed for the kitchen, he had Jacy's door key in his pocket. She was going to have one hell of a time kicking him out once she pulled herself together enough to try to do it.

Jacy ate two burritos, spoke little and fled to take a shower as soon as she finished eating. Tabor arrived when she was barely dry. Tom let him in, then set his laptop computer on her table and worked on a report, giving her a degree of privacy while she talked to her boss. He didn't even listen in...much.

He heard enough to know she was on indefinite medical leave.

Staying away from the job she loved wasn't going to be easy for her. Tom knew that much, though he was beginning to realize there was one hell of a lot he didn't know about the woman who was carrying his baby. A few months ago he would have said Jacy wasn't capable of putting anything or anyone ahead of her career.

He knew better now. He'd seen her last night, when she thought she might lose the baby.

When Tabor stood to leave, he spoke to Tom. "Want to walk downstairs with me, Rasmussin?"

Their eyes met. Tom read the other man's intentions easily. Jacy didn't have any family to look after her, but apparently she did have friends who would stand up for her. Tom found he was pleased to learn that. He nodded and hit a couple of keys, saving his work.

Jacy groaned. "No, Tabor. You promised."

"I didn't call him," the older man said mildly.

"You're determined to embarrass me, aren't you?"

"It's all right," Tom said, shutting off his laptop as he stood.

"No, it isn't." Jacy sat on the red couch, her legs tucked up, looking aggrieved and luscious. The loose, swingy shirt she wore had wide yellow-and-white stripes and ended at her waist, concealing what Tom knew were splendid breasts. Her snug white shorts bared every inch of her long legs. Tom's mouth went dry when he looked at her.

"The two of you," she said firmly, "are not going to sneak out of here and play macho man games, do you hear?"

He smiled, dry-mouthed and aching as he crossed the room to stand next to the couch and torment himself by looking down at her. "You're cute when you pout."

Her eyes went wide with outrage. "I do not—"

He bent quickly and dropped a light kiss on her mouth. "I'll be back in a minute."

The kiss had been a mistake, he decided as he closed the door behind him. No matter how much he'd enjoyed astonishing Jacy into silence, it had been a mistake. Even that casual taste of her was too much.

Damn, he was obsessed, wasn't he? Or maybe masochistic. He was hard and aching from one look at her legs, one brief taste of her mouth, and there wasn't a damn thing he could do about it for at least a week. Maybe a lot longer. Like the next seven months or so.

"We've run into each other a time or two over the years," Tabor said, taking the stairs one slow step at a time. He used his cane on one side and the railing on the other to steady himself. "I don't claim to know you well, Rasmussin, but what I do know I've respected."

"Until now?" Tom asked dryly. He held himself to Tabor's slow pace. The stairs were bound to be hell on the man's knees, but he'd come to see Jacy anyway, when he could have called or sent someone or both. Tom had respected Tabor before. Now, he thought he was beginning to like him. "Did you come here to talk to Jacy, or to check me out?"

"No reason I can't do both, is there?"

"I guess not," Tom said, and with those words conceded Tabor's right to question him about Jacy.

"I know you've been Jacy's cop for the last year or so. She's gotten a few tips from you, passed you some information."

They were almost to the landing. "Yeah, we've worked together awhile now."

"I also know you hurt her." Tabor reached the landing and turned to face Tom. The skin on his face was taut— maybe from pain. Maybe from anger. "Not that she confided in me. Jacy's too used to being alone to do that, but I know her. She'd been unhappy the past couple months, deep-down unhappy. I didn't know why until I learned about her pregnancy."

Tom sucked a breath in. "I didn't intend to hurt her. I...made a mistake."

"Don't make any more."

Tabor was a tall man, tall enough to look Tom in the eyes, but he was also over sixty and half-crippled. The threat in his voice might have seemed ludicrous. Tom met the judgment in those hard brown eyes and didn't feel the least amused. "I won't make the same mistake again," he said quietly. "But I can't promise never to hurt her."

"Do you love her?"

Anger surged in from nowhere, a confusing force, fierce and directionless, that swept over him in a wave. "I like her. I respect her." *I want her so badly I don't know how I'm going to stay sane when I don't dare touch her.*

"That's not what I asked."

As swiftly and unreasonably as it had hit, Tom's anger receded. He clenched his fists against the undertow. "I don't know what the hell I feel, all right?"

"Are you going to marry her?"

"Yes," Tom said, because this much he was sure of.

The other man's eyebrows went up in surprise or disbelief. "She's agreed?"

"No. But she will."

Five

Jacy had spent thirty-one years building a life and an identity for herself. She'd had help along the way—help from people like Sister Mary Elizabeth when she was small. Help from friends like Tabor when she was older. But growing up without family, without any hint of who or what she came from, meant she'd pretty much invented herself.

Her clever invention lay in pieces at her feet now. Reporting had always been more than a job to her. She'd known that the world was not a safe place since she was too small to put it into words; the good guys didn't always win, and bad things really did happen to good people.

All anyone could really count on was themselves. In such a world, information was essential. People needed facts on which to base the daily choices of their lives, facts about the changing world around them. Jacy had her share of personal ambition, but in a secret place deep inside she'd always felt she'd been called to reporting almost the way a priest is called to the priesthood.

Now she couldn't work.

Jacy's stereo was in her living room, but her TV was in her bedroom. After Tabor left she spent the afternoon holed up in there, watching Wally and the Beaver, Lassie, Donna Reed and Sergeant Joe Friday. She wasn't looking for answers. She didn't even know what the questions were yet. She just needed to be somewhere else for a while. Someplace where things made sense.

Tom knocked on her door once, to tell her he was going to the grocery store. When he knocked again, the sun had started its slide down the western edge of the world. "You awake in there?" he called through the door. "Supper's almost ready."

Jacy sat in her queen-size bed with the covers all jumbled. Her knees were drawn up, her head pillowed on them. Black and white images flickered on the television screen.

Tom had been decent, more than decent, about everything so far. She wished he'd quit it. She wanted to keep thinking of him as the sorry SOB she'd convinced herself he was. "You can open the door," she said. "I'm almost finished feeling sorry for myself."

He opened the door, which she'd invited him to do, and came in, which she hadn't. "Have you always been this hard on yourself," he asked, "and I just didn't notice?"

She looked at him standing in her bedroom, only a few feet from her bed, and grimaced. "You know, I need to remember that you're one of those give-'em-an-inch-and-they'll-take-a-mile types."

He smiled. It was a slow, comfortable smile, not consciously sexy, and it made the breath catch in her chest.

Oh, Lord, she thought, looking away. *I'm in trouble.* "Something smells good."

"Spaghetti sauce." His voice was closer. "I'll get the pasta cooking in a minute. I hope you like garlic."

Damn him, damn him, how could he do this? How could he stand here in her bedroom, next to the bed where he'd taken her to places she hadn't known existed, and sound so blasted normal? She swallowed.

"I've laid you down in that bed twice," he said suddenly, his voice husky. "Last night you were asleep. The time before that, we started a baby."

Her head turned sharply.

He was looking straight at her. Flames burned in those pale eyes. "I remember everything, Jacy. I remember how you moved under my hands, how you tasted. The way you whimpered when I ran my tongue up your belly. I've tried to forget, but I can't."

"And you didn't call me afterward," she said, her head held high and her sarcasm thick enough to hide behind, "because you were so concerned for my feelings."

He watched her in silence for a moment that stretched out too long, a moment taut with the force that sang between them. "No," he said at last. "I wanted to think so, but I guess I was mostly selfish." His mouth quirked up on one side, but no smile lit the bleakness in his eyes. "You scared me pretty bad that night, you know." He turned and started for the door.

"Tom..."

He looked back at her.

She had no idea why she'd spoken. She'd wanted to say his name. Just that. Just his name. Her mind was blank of everything else.

"We've got a lot to settle," he said softly. "But we've got time. I'm not leaving this time."

She shivered. For some reason that sounded more like a threat than a promise.

Tom's mother was nothing like Jacy had pictured her.

After all, Jacy knew both of Lydia Rasmussin's sons by the time the woman called on Thursday and asked if she could come over. So Jacy was expecting someone with either Raz's charm or Tom's intensity.

Not that she knew Raz well, but when Tom had gone into work on Monday at Jacy's insistence, he'd asked his brother to check on her. Raz's hours as an undercover cop were erratic, but he tended to work evenings more than daytimes. He'd dropped by every day, and Jacy thought they were on their way to becoming friends. She hoped so. It was good to think at least one member of Tom's family accepted her and the baby.

Jacy's first impression when she opened the door that afternoon was that someone had shrunk June Cleaver and dyed her hair dark. Lydia Rasmussin was a delicate, soft-spoken woman who might have been able to claim a full inch over five feet—but Jacy doubted it. She had happy lines around her eyes and mouth, the kind a person gets from years of smiles, and she gave the impression of a person who used to be shy but has learned, over the years, to overcome it.

Jacy liked her. She just didn't know what to say to her. That was disconcerting for a woman who'd chatted with diplomats and serial killers in the course of interviews. But Lydia was a woman who liked to talk about family. They talked about Raz briefly, and a cousin of Tom's who'd recently moved back to South Texas with his new wife, but Jacy couldn't contribute much to such a discussion.

It didn't help that Lydia obviously felt as uncomfortable as Jacy did.

They sat in Jacy's living room, Lydia on the striped chair, Jacy on the red couch, and made awkward conversation over the coffee and cookies Tom's mother had brought. She'd brought a chicken casserole, too. It was in the oven now, waiting on Tom to return from work.

"These cookies are delicious," Jacy said. She reached for another gooey chocolate chip fat-bomb.

"I wasn't sure if I should bring them," Lydia said, fiddling nervously with the handle of her coffee mug. Her nails were painted a pale pink, and her only jewelry was her gold wedding band. "From what Tom told me, I had the impression you prefer healthy foods."

"Sometimes, but I'm crazy about chocolate." Jacy would have given a lot to know just what Tom had told his parents about her. She grinned suddenly, remembering the man she'd gotten to know before she made the mistake of going to bed with him. "Are you sure he didn't just call me a jock?"

Lydia blinked, then laughed and set down her coffee cup. "As a matter of fact, he did. I'm being ridiculous, aren't I? I promise you, I'm not usually so stuffy." She shook her head, amused with herself. "I'll confess to being old-fashioned enough to be uncomfortable with the idea of you two living together, but you'd think my son was fourteen, not forty, the way I'm acting."

"Well," Jacy said, feeling the clutch of nerves in her stomach. "It is an awkward situation. You probably hadn't ever heard my name before he told you I was pregnant. It's bound to be something of a shock. May I ask you something?"

"Of course."

"When did Tom tell you about the baby?"

"Last night."

Jacy tried not to feel hurt. She didn't know how families operated, and it was probably hard for a man to tell his mother he'd gotten some woman pregnant.

But she'd come home from the hospital five days ago. That seemed like more than enough time.

"I appreciate you letting me come over like this, Jacy," the other woman was saying. "Tom wanted to wait until you were back on your feet before introducing us, and perhaps I was selfish, rushing over here like this." She smiled. "I guess he knows me pretty well. He waited until you were feeling better before he told me, didn't he? I suspect he knew I'd make a beeline over here."

Jacy shrugged, uncomfortable. "I guess. Are you happy about the baby, then?"

"My dear, I'm sixty-two years old. I'd begun to wonder if either of my sons was ever going to make me a grand-mother. I'm delirious."

Jacy took a sip of her own coffee so she could study the woman sitting in the brightly striped chair. She suspected Lydia Rasmussin's feelings were a good deal more mixed than she was admitting, but Jacy believed the woman meant what she said. Like Sister Mary Elizabeth used to say, sometimes it really is the thought that counts.

Thinking of the nun eased Jacy even as it brought a pang of guilt. She still hadn't told Sister Mary Elizabeth about the baby. But she didn't want to do it over the phone, and she couldn't travel yet. "Well, that's good." She smiled, too. "I'm glad my baby will have a grandmother."

"I'm glad, too. And not just about the baby. I must ad-mit, I never thought Tom would marry again. And you're so very different from…" The shadow of old grief crossed the other woman's face. She shook her head. "I'm sorry. No doubt it's best that you are so unlike Allison."

Jacy went very still. "Mrs. Rasmussin," she said care-fully, "did Tom tell you we were getting married?"

"Not exactly." She looked uncertain. "He said he'd asked you, but nothing was settled. I assumed…I thought he meant you hadn't set a date yet."

Nothing was settled. Anger bunched in Jacy's middle like a fist. "He asked," she said tersely. "I turned him down."

"Oh. I see." But it was obvious from her expression that she didn't understand at all. Nor did she approve, though she was trying to conceal her dismay.

"I'm sorry." Jacy wanted to tell the older woman that her son was sleeping on the couch, not in her bed. Yes, Tom wanted her. Sometimes she caught him watching her, his eyes hungry and waiting. That didn't matter. It didn't matter that her body reacted when she felt those pale eyes on her, either. She had no intention of allowing him back into her bed. Ever.

"I don't plan to marry," she said instead. "But *I* do want my child to have grandparents. I want him or her to have family."

"Well." She fiddled with her coffee cup some more. "I can't say I'm comfortable with your decision, but it is your decision, not mine." Her smile was tentative. "You said 'him or her.' I take it you haven't had a sonogram yet? Or is it just too early to tell?"

"Both, really. I was supposed to get a sonogram on my next appointment, but with everything that's happened, I've decided to change doctors. I want one with more experience. I've been researching my condition, looking into who in this area is most familiar with it, and I've got an appointment with a Dr. Robbins next Monday. I think he's planning a sonogram as part of the exam."

"Sometimes," the other woman said almost shyly, "they let you have a picture, a copy of the sonogram. Do you think you—"

The sound of a key turning in the door made her break off. Both women turned to look as Tom swung the door open and stepped inside.

He shook his head when he saw his mother. "I should have known. Mom, I asked you not to rush over here and play twenty questions."

"Nonsense," Lydia said, standing. "I only asked two or three." She walked over to the tall, scowling man who was her son and slipped one arm around him for a hug. Tom's face softened in a way Jacy had never seen before as he looked down at his mother.

That's what he looks like with someone he loves. The thought came into her head fully formed. Jacy pushed it away. "Lydia brought over a casserole. It's in the oven."

"Southwest chicken," he said, his arm going around the

tiny woman at his side. "I smelled it the second I stepped inside. If you think you can bribe me with my favorite dish—"

"Of course I can," she said, laughing.

Jacy watched as Tom walked his mother to the door, the two of them smiling and finishing each other's sentences. The top of Lydia's head didn't reach Tom's shoulder and their features were nothing alike, yet their kinship was obvious.

They loved each other, yes. They also enjoyed each other.

Envy was a sharp, green sliver that had lodged in Jacy's throat years ago. She felt it now with every breath. *My baby won't have to wonder what family feels like,* she told herself. Her baby would be part of that warmth.

Lydia Rasmussin turned at the door, and she and Jacy said the appropriate things to each other. Then she left, and Jacy and Tom were alone.

"You told her we were getting married," she said, gathering her anger around herself protectively.

"I wondered what was bothering you. No, I didn't tell her we were getting married. I said I'd asked you, but nothing was settled."

"Well, she assumed that meant we just hadn't set the date yet! Dammit, Tom, why didn't you just tell her you'd done your duty and I turned you down? Do you have any idea how awkward I felt?"

He sighed. "My mother is of a different generation. She doesn't really understand the idea that being a single mother is somehow better than marrying the father of your child. Frankly," he said, heading for the kitchen, "I don't, either."

"What does that mean?" Frustration boiled up in Jacy hot and fast. She wanted to move, to pace, and was trapped on the couch. Four more days, she told herself. In four more days she'd see the doctor and surely, surely some of the restrictions would be lifted.

"It means that I intend for our child to have two parents who live together, and I'm a conventional man. For me, that means marriage." He disappeared into the kitchen. "Did you really think that because you turned me down once, the subject was closed?"

Yes, that's what she'd thought, what she'd needed to think. "The subject *is* closed." She wanted so badly to follow him, grab him, shake some sense into his thick head. She wanted...more than she was willing to think about. "You can't stay here if you're going to start pressuring me about marriage, Rasmussin."

He came back out with a can of beer in his hand and looked at her coolly. "You're itching for a fight, aren't you? I guess an argument might be an improvement over the way you've hidden away in your room ever since I moved in."

Her lip lifted in a sneer. "I'm sorry you've been dissatisfied with my company."

"Oh, I've enjoyed your company just fine, when you've deigned to share a few minutes with me over supper."

Jacy had enjoyed those minutes, too. She'd begun to look forward to them, to the conversations shared along with the meal, the sort of talks they used to enjoy sometimes over drinks. So far, about the only things they agreed on were fifties' rock, the Astros' chances and the frustration of dealing with bureaucracies—but disagreeing was more fun, anyway.

Only, dammit, she didn't want to spend her days waiting for Tom to come home. It made her feel pathetic. "Just because you're living here temporarily doesn't give you any claims on me. If you want company, go find some."

He got tight all over without changing expression. "That's it." He set his beer down on the table. "We'd better get a few things straight. I've let you avoid—"

"Let me? You've *let* me?" Anger felt good. Really good. She leaned forward, stabbing the air with her finger. "Let me tell you something. You do not have what it takes to *let* me do anything."

Something moved in his pale eyes, something dark and almost frightening. "I guess we'll talk later," he said, and started toward her.

She sat up straighter. "What are you doing?"

"Nothing you don't want. Nothing you aren't damned near begging for—though I suppose you'll make me pay for that comment." He slid his knee onto the couch, bent over her and seized her chin in one hard hand, tipping her face up. "But later," he said, his voice growing softer, deeper, with each word. "Make me pay later, Jacy." Her name was no more than a hot breath across her lips as his mouth claimed hers.

Tom knew he was in trouble the moment he felt her mouth beneath his. If he'd meant to teach Jacy that she needed him, that she couldn't taunt him by day and haunt him at night without paying the price, he defeated himself in that first second.

She tasted like spring and freedom, like every hungry adolescent dream he'd ever had. She slid into his bloodstream like summer—hot, languid and compelling. When she tried to pull her head back, to pull away from him, he groaned and trapped her in place with his other hand behind her neck.

He nipped at her lower lip. Her mouth opened to him, and he came inside.

A shudder traveled up her body. He felt it, though he touched her nowhere but her mouth, her face, her neck. Then she moved—but not away from him. Her body lifted toward him. Her hand slid up his chest, lingering, caressing. And he knew which of them was ready to beg. "Jacy," he whispered against her lips, his own hands still, his body rigid. "Let me touch you. Please. I need to touch you."

She shifted, moving over on the couch. Making room for him. He needed no more invitation to bring them together, body to body.

She pressed against him and hunger clawed at his gut. He was raw with need—with more than one kind of need. He had to be careful, had to be sure he didn't hurt her. Not this time. Her hands made it hard to balance his need to possess with his need to protect—such busy hands, as eager for his body as he was for hers. Their mouths clung together while their fingers tugged at this and unfastened that, while their bodies strained against each other.

She had his shirt unbuttoned and pulled free from his pants before he managed to find the zipper on her dress and lower it enough to pull her dress down on one side. She wore lace beneath her clothes, lace the color of peaches. The breast so nearly bared to him was full and beautiful, and he couldn't wait. He bent and kissed her nipple through the lace.

Jacy cried out.

The lace was rough to his tongue. The flesh beneath it was hot. He licked, then sucked.

She gasped his name, her hand clutching and releasing his hair as rhythmically as his mouth suckled her. She was so responsive. He knew if he slid his hand between her legs he'd find her already wet and ready for him, and the knowledge was killing him. But he couldn't touch her there. Not yet.

"Tom," she said again, her voice thin with need. "Tom, the baby. We can't. The baby."

He raised his face to look into her eyes, huge, passion-drowned eyes. "I won't hurt the baby, Jacy. I won't do anything that could hurt the baby." He was going to hurt himself. He accepted that. The pain and frustration would be worth it for these moments of holding her, touching her, watching her come apart for him.

He meant to see it happen this time. When he'd had her

before, her bedroom had been nearly dark, with only a little light filtering in from the living room. He couldn't have her this time, not completely, but at least he would watch her when he sent her up the peak, and over.

His hand shook when he pulled down the wet lace of her bra, leaving her breast naked. He pleasured her with his tongue, with his teeth, until his control stretched too tight and the frantic motions of her body told him she was near the edge. Then, at last, he let his hand slide up her bare leg, up under the thin material of her dress.

His fingers were almost touching her center when her body suddenly contorted—away from him. "No." She pushed at him—pushed his head away from her breast, pushed his hand away. "No, Tom!"

Bemused, not understanding, he lifted his head. "I promised not to hurt the baby," he said softly. "I'm just going to touch you, Jacy. I won't take you. Let me do this for you."

The flush of arousal mantled her cheeks, her breast. Her lips were moist and swollen, parted to let out her shallow breaths…and her eyes were the frantic green of a hurricane sky. "No," she said. "I can't. I won't. Not because of the baby. I don't trust you, Tom. I can't let you do that to me when I don't trust you."

Tom looked at the rejection on her face, and fear brushed against him like the first frost of fall—a touch of ice, chilly and threatening. Some damage couldn't be fixed. Some hurts couldn't be forgiven, and some mistakes, he knew, were forever.

Tom paused in the doorway to take off his hat, shaking raindrops from the black felt. It was a thoroughly gray Monday outside, with rain drizzling down from colorless skies.

Inside, Tom's presence in the crowded waiting room drew the immediate attention of every person in the room.

And every person in the room, except for him and the receptionist, was pregnant.

In the course of his job over the past twenty years, Tom had talked to witnesses in tenements where rats fought with the roaches over spoiled food. He'd questioned suspects in their private jets and in the cardboard boxes in the alley they called home. He'd arrested a clown at a Halloween party, and a woman at her daughter's wedding.

Never had he felt quite so thoroughly out of place.

A faint, embarrassed heat crept up his cheeks. He strode forward, his hat in his hand. "I'm Tom Rasmussin," he told the receptionist. "Is my…is Jacy James here?"

"Of course, Lieutenant. I remember. You brought your medical history in last Thursday and let us have a little blood, didn't you?" She smiled a bright, professional smile.

"Have they done the sonogram yet? Can I join her?"

"I'm afraid you missed the sonogram, and Dr. Robbins is with Ms. James now. If you'll have a seat, she should be out shortly."

Damn, he thought, bitterly disappointed. He found a chair that sat by itself in one corner, flanked by a tall green plant on one side and a table strewn with magazines on the other, and sat to wait. He knew he was late, well past the time he was supposed to meet Jacy here, but he'd hoped the doctor hadn't been able to see her yet. Dr. Robbins was working Jacy in between his regular appointments.

Apparently the doctor was running more nearly on time than Tom was today. He sighed and settled his damp hat on his knee.

No doubt he was in trouble for failing to show up when he said he would. Not that he'd had much choice. All hell had broken loose that morning on what should have been a routine arrest. Briefly, images of blood and violence flowed through Tom's mind; with an act of will, he shut them away.

They'd be back, he knew. He didn't expect to get much sleep tonight.

But he knew better than to offer the demands of his job as an excuse for not being here. He couldn't very well tell a pregnant woman exactly what had happened to delay him. All Jacy would know was that he'd honored the demands of his job ahead of his obligation to her. He didn't expect a woman to understand that.

Allison never had. It had always hurt her when he put police work first. If she'd been here today instead of Jacy, she'd have spent the next couple of days looking at him reproachfully every so often and waiting for him to figure out how—

Tom blinked, shocked and guilty. It seemed profoundly wrong, disloyal, to think of Allison and Jacy at the same time. Yet he wasn't sure which of them he was being disloyal to.

The uncertainty made the guilt worse.

He clenched his jaw and looked around, hoping for distraction. Ever since Jacy had told him about the baby he'd been noticing how full of pregnant women Houston was. About half of them seemed to be in the waiting room with him that morning.

The table beside him held a scattering of magazines, including one on parenting that he'd seen Jacy reading at the apartment. It had a mother and baby on the cover. He hesitated, then picked it up.

When Jacy returned to the waiting room it was even more crowded than it had been earlier, but she had no trouble spotting Tom tucked away in the corner. He wasn't the only man there—a couple of daddies-to-be had shown up since she'd gone in to be examined. But he was far and away the most compelling.

She wasn't the only one who thought so, either. Tom's attention was on the magazine he was reading, so he didn't notice the frequent glances he drew from several of the women in the room. Jacy did. The feeling of possessiveness those glances stirred in her was both new and unsettling.

He did notice Jacy, though. As soon as she started across the room toward him his head came up. He stood, and their gazes met.

Sometimes in the past when Jacy's eyes had met Tom's, she'd had an odd feeling, as if his eyes were speaking to her in a language she couldn't understand, but ought to. That feeling swept over her now—a sense that meanings pressed at the backs of his eyes, the fluid and concrete set of meanings that made up Tom Rasmussin.

She broke eye contact, shaken. Good grief. She was really losing it. Next she'd be thinking she could read his mind or something.

"So how are you?" Tom asked softly when she reached him.

"Fine, I guess. I haven't really talked to Dr. Robbins yet. He wanted to run his tests and do the exam before he talked to me—to us, I mean. It may be a little while."

"I wanted to be here," he told her. "I'm sorry I was late. I missed seeing the sonogram done."

His apology made her feel skittish. She'd wanted him there, too. She'd been disappointed when he hadn't made it, and she didn't like feeling that way. Jacy shrugged. "We knew you might have trouble keeping the appointment. That's why I got a friend to drop me off instead of waiting for you to pick me up. It doesn't matter."

"You probably didn't much want me here, anyway. But I'm still sorry."

He'd apologized twice. It wasn't like him. There was a tightness to his voice, too, a drawn look around his eyes. Abruptly she forgot to worry about her own feelings. "What happened? Something went wrong, didn't it? You said all you had was a routine bust this morning."

"It should have been."

"So what went wrong?"

He grimaced and ran a hand over his hair. "Jacy, you don't need to hear about it, believe me."

She frowned at him impatiently. "Come on, Tom, I've covered the crime beat in Houston for five years. Maybe I'm not a cop, but there isn't a lot I haven't seen."

He got a startled look in his eyes, as if she'd said something completely unexpected. But that made no sense. He knew what she did for a living, and what that entailed. "Tom?" she said, puzzled.

"I'd be pretty stupid if I tried to protect you from the sorts of things that have made up your job the past few years, wouldn't I?" he said slowly.

"You said it, not me."

His mustache twitched in a half smile, but his eyes had the same considering look. As if she'd sprouted a second head or something.

"Well?" she demanded. "Are you going to tell me what happened this morning? And quit looking at me as if I had broccoli between my teeth."

His smile deepened. "Later, maybe, I'll tell you. I don't think this is the place for me to go into detail. And you're not supposed to be on your feet."

She glanced around. Both of the women closest to them looked as though they were listening as hard as they could while pretending to be reading their magazines. No, these nice ladies probably didn't need to hear about whatever horror made Tom's eyes so tight and flat.

"You're right on both counts," she said, and promptly sat in the chair he'd been in.

That surprised a chuckle out of him. "First time that's happened—you admitting I'm right."

"The occasion hasn't arisen before," she said dryly.

He stood in front of her chair, turning his hat over in his hands and looking tall, dark and rather charmingly awkward. "I guess I'll go find a seat myself."

"Wait a minute." Impulsively she reached out, laying

her hand on his arm. He felt warm and solid beneath the crisp cotton of his shirt. "What you said earlier about me not wanting you here—that wasn't true."

"No?"

She picked her words carefully. "I know you wanted to be here, and I guess it would have been nice if you'd been able to make it. And I'm sorry you missed the sonogram, too. It was pretty special. But they took pictures."

The look in his eyes—pleasure, and something beyond pleasure—made her glad she'd told him. He crouched beside her chair. "Could they tell if it's a boy or a girl?"

She laughed. "Not really. The pictures are fuzzy, and things aren't clearly developed yet, if you know what I mean. But I could see little toes and fingers. And it moved. I saw it move." Her hand slid over her stomach as she remembered the wonder.

"It moved?" He took a step closer and crouched beside her chair. "You saw the baby move? Can you feel it moving now?"

She shook her head. "Not yet. Not for another four to six weeks, according to my books, but it's already moving, even if I can't feel it."

He stared at her stomach, his gaze as intent as if he might be able to see through the skin and muscle to where their baby rested if he just concentrated hard enough. "You don't look any different."

But she was. In small, significant ways her body was changing. "The baby is so tiny still," she said, "only about two-and-a-half inches long. I haven't gained much weight yet, so the changes aren't very noticeable."

His eyes came up to hers. "Your breasts are bigger," he said softly.

She blushed. She could hardly believe it, but she did blush.

"Ms. James?" the nurse's voice broke in. "If you and

Lieutenant Rasmussin would like to step back to the doctor's office, he'll be with you in a few minutes.''

They followed the nurse down the hall. Jacy was painfully aware of the man walking beside her. She reassured herself that at least she'd figured out what her problem was, the reason she felt this man's presence along her skin like an electric current.

Hormones. A woman's body gets hormonally charged during pregnancy, making emotions stronger, closer to the surface.

Some women responded to the hormonal overload by crying a lot. Some became irritable. Last night it had dawned on her that she'd reacted by lusting after Tom.

Probably she would be getting equally excited about any decent-looking male who was, well, *available* right now. Especially if he were built like Tom, with the lean efficiency of a wolf. Especially if he moved with the rangy grace of that animal. Especially if he kept watching her as if...

Jacy glanced at Tom as they reached the door to the doctor's office. He stood aside, waiting for her to go in first...watching her with the patient hunger of a predator stalking its prey.

She shivered and went through the door. With luck, he wouldn't be so blasted available after today. Once the doctor gave her permission to be on her feet again, she wouldn't need Tom anymore.

Six

"**Y**ou just can't stand to admit that you need me, can you?" Tom demanded.

"I don't need you," Jacy said, staring straight ahead. The windshield wipers swished back and forth, back and forth—repetitive, monotonous, hypnotic.

"Jacy," he said almost gently, "the news wasn't that bad."

"He couldn't give me a firm prognosis without any family history."

"He also said the baby's fine. And he asked you if you'd ever tried tracking down the identity of your mother." Tom glanced at her and signaled a turn. "You're a reporter. You're used to digging into records, solving puzzles. So why haven't you ever tried to solve this one? It might not be that hard if you were born here. How many babies born in Houston thirty-one years ago were named Jacinta Caitlin?"

She shifted uncomfortably. Her last name had been

picked by someone at the orphanage. Her first and second names came from the note pinned to the blanket someone's hands had tucked around her before leaving her on the orphanage steps. "Her name is Jacinta Caitlin," the note had said.

When she was small, she'd treasured that name because it was the one thing she was sure came from her mother. When she grew older and less naive—when she stopped fantasizing about the woman who had borne her—she'd asked to be called by her initials. J.C. had quickly become Jacy. No one but Sister Mary Elizabeth had called her Jacinta in years.

"Dr. Robbins doesn't *have* to know about her," she told Tom. *And neither do I.*

They stopped at the light. "True. He was pretty optimistic about you being able to carry the baby full-term."

"That's right. So I can take care of myself again. I expect you to have your things moved out by tonight."

The light changed. He muttered something under his breath and made the turn onto Oak Street. Her heart was beating hard and quick, twice as fast as the measured sweep of the wipers. Almost frantic. They were almost home... *But the apartment is home for me,* she thought, *not for him. He's temporary.*

"What are you going to do for money for the next year or so if I move out?"

"I've got savings. I can work awhile longer, too, part-time. Dr. Robbins said that as long as I get plenty of sleep at night I can be up for three hours at a stretch." Three hours up followed by one hour horizontal, with eight hours' sleep each night and limited exercise—those were the rules for her now.

He made a skeptical noise. "What are you going to do—stop in the middle of covering a drive-by and stretch out in your car when your three hours are up?" He shook his head. "And how long will you be able to work even part-time? As the pregnancy progresses you'll be able to spend less and less time on your feet."

"I've got savings," she repeated.

"Be reasonable, Jacy. You're not going to be able to support yourself. Let me."

Let him support her? Depend on him for everything from the roof over her head to—to things she didn't intend to contemplate. "I want you out. Tonight. You have to move out tonight."

Tom was silent for the last block. Silent as he pulled into the apartment parking lot and parked in the empty space beside her Mustang. Then he turned to her, his expression grim. "You can't bring yourself to trust me at all, can you? Yes, I'm the bastard who walked out on you. But I didn't lie to you. I don't break my promises, Jacy. I give you my word I won't abandon you and the baby."

Jacy wanted to argue, wanted to tell him she wouldn't trust him to pay a parking ticket for her, much less be responsible for her and her baby.

She wanted to lie. To both of them. "Oh, damn," she said softly, and leaned her head back against the headrest. "It's me, not you. I can't stand to be dependent. Not on anyone. It makes me crazy, as if—don't some animals gnaw their own legs off if they get caught in a trap?"

She turned her head away, looking out the window instead. Her cherry red Mustang sat next to them, the hood all shiny with rain. Jacy had spent three years getting that car restored, getting things done a little at a time. It was a classic, in top condition.

Tom shut off the ignition, leaving them in silence except for the hushed sound of the rain outside. "Jacy."

She looked at her Mustang now and wondered how much she could get for it. If she added that to what she had in savings, would it be enough?

"Jacy," Tom said again.

Slowly, reluctantly, she faced him.

"Some animals, when caught in a trap, have been known to gnaw their legs off. But they bleed to death."

That was all he said—no pleading, no demands. He didn't tell her she carried his child and that gave him a say in what she decided. He didn't repeat all the sensible things he'd said so far. He just sat there looking at her with his cop's face—an expression that held little enough hope or compromise, but a surprising amount of compassion.

She could choose to deny Tom's help, and she would probably bleed to death financially. He knew it. So did she. If she were the only one who would be hurt by her actions, she'd probably do just that. But she wasn't alone anymore. She had to be strong and smart enough for two now.

She was terrified. "You could support me without living with me."

"No," he said, "I can't. Lord, Jacy, you did that series on the proposed budget cuts last summer. You know what cops earn."

"You're a detective. A lieutenant. You've been on the force for twenty years."

He snorted.

And he was right. She knew better.

His voice was very gentle when he spoke again. "Jacy, even if I move out now I'll have to move in again—maybe next month, maybe not for several months, but you're going to spend more time in bed as the baby gets bigger and heavier. You're going to need someone to take care of you."

The trap was swinging shut on her. "I don't want to be badgered about marriage. I don't want to hear about it."

"Is that a condition? All right. If it will make you feel better, I won't ask you to marry me again while I'm living with you. But that doesn't mean I'm giving up on the idea."

The rain had dwindled while they talked. It was a heavy mist now, damp and gray and good for little more than covering the sun. She swallowed, grabbed the cage door with both hands…and pulled it closed. "All right," she said. "I guess you'll want to sublease your apartment or something."

"Or something," he agreed. "But then, so will you."

She had to move.

It hadn't occurred to her until Tom mentioned it. Jacy felt foolish for overlooking the obvious. Her apartment only had one bedroom, so she would have had to move when the baby came, or soon after, anyway.

To have room for Tom in the months to come, she'd have to move sooner, that was all. He needed a room and a bed. He hadn't complained about sleeping on her couch, but she couldn't expect him to keep that up indefinitely.

If panic tickled at the back of her mind at the thought of yet another change, she ignored it. That afternoon, while Tom was at work, she called her apartment manager, and she lucked out. Another unit would be available in ten days, a two-bedroom, town-house-style apartment.

She and Tom were very reasonable, very civilized when they discussed the move that night at supper. He wasn't picky about where he lived, he said. She didn't mind if he wanted to blend a few of his things with hers, she said.

Because Jacy was used to throwing herself at whatever scared her, she insisted on making the arrangements herself, but she made the mistake of telling Nan about the move. That's when she lost control.

When Tom came home two days later, the apartment smelled of some happy blend of food and spice. He closed the front door, took his hat off and set down the briefcase that held the results of his latest investigation—a very personal investigation.

It had been a long time since he'd been greeted after work by the smell of supper cooking.

His mother was a traditional homemaker. She believed in hot food and plenty of it for her family. Allison, too, had loved to cook, to play with recipes, creating fancy dishes that were sometimes ruined by the time he made it home. Tom stood just inside Jacy's door now and waited for the grief or the guilt to hit.

But the feeling that slipped over him had nothing to do with guilt, and was only faintly tinged with sadness. Tom had no name for what he felt as he stood there with his briefcase in one hand, his hat in the other. It simply rolled over him, as delicate as dawn, as sweet as homecoming. He felt like a kid waking up on a birthday morning...only he was an adult, a man who had been out in the cold a long time.

Too long. He hadn't wanted to come in, and the warmth hurt as much as it compelled.

He followed his nose to the kitchen.

Jacy stood at the sink, rinsing lettuce. Her slacks and shirt were made of some crinkly material. One was royal blue, the other a bright yellow.

The wonderful smells were coming from a slow-cooker on the counter next to her. "I didn't know you cooked," he said.

"You knew I ate." She glanced over her shoulder at him. Maybe there was pleasure mixed with the wariness in her eyes. He wanted to think so. "I figured out years ago that if I wanted to eat anything but fast food I'd better learn how to fix it."

Months ago, when they were eating chips and salsa with their beer and arguing over who owed whom information, she'd told him what she usually did for supper. After eating junk all day she'd go home and throw some veggies in the steamer. There was a big difference in Tom's mind between steaming a handful of vegetables and really cooking.

He lifted the glass lid on the pot and fragrant steam poufed out. "Soup?"

"Mmm-hmm. It's sort of Italian." She gave him another quick glance. "You seem to like Italian."

He smiled. "You mean because I fixed us spaghetti twice in the past week and brought home pizza once, you think I like Italian food?"

She smiled. Jacy's face was lovely when she was grouchy or tired; when she smiled all-out this way, she took his breath away. "That was a clue."

Her smile fed something in Tom, a place where more than one appetite joined in a heady mix. Jacy had cooked for him. She might deny it if asked straight-out, but she'd cooked this for him. Satisfaction, deep and rich, broadened his smile. "I'm crazy about Italian," he said. "Need any help?"

She told him he could get the bread from the oven and dish out the soup while she finished the salads.

It should have been simple enough to do. Tom had made himself at home in her kitchen the past ten days. But it was such a *small* kitchen.

She brushed against him when she crossed to the refrigerator, and his body came to attention. A moment later he straightened as he closed the oven door, holding the hot bread with a dish towel. He turned. She was reaching for the grater on the top shelf, and they connected again, hip to hip this time. Her breath caught audibly.

Dr. Robbins had given Jacy the green light on more than one sort of activity. He'd said that sex was permissible at this time, too. What had been frustratingly impossible two days ago was all too possible now, and they both knew it.

After two seconds of heart-pounding silence, she moved away and started grating Parmesan on their salads.

Tom let her. He studied her for a moment, his heartbeat hard and insistent. She didn't look at him. Her hands weren't steady. He nodded to himself and left to put the bread on the dining table. When he came back she was putting the grater in the dishwasher. He walked up to her.

She turned. He laid his hand on her hip and felt the quick jerk of her muscles from alarm—or delight. Her eyes went wide. She was warm and firm beneath his hand, beautifully curved as he ran his hand slowly up her body.

She stopped him with her hand as he neared her breast. "No."

"Why not?" He looked at her flushed face. Her lips were parted. Her eyes held equal parts arousal and confusion, and he ached for her so badly he could hardly keep his hand from shaking. "I like touching you, Jacy." He shifted his hand away from the area she was forbidding him and caressed her waist. "You like it, too."

"It doesn't matter," she said a little desperately, and stepped away. "You promised—"

"I promised not to mention marriage." He smiled slowly. "I'm not asking you for marriage tonight. Let me touch you. Kiss you."

"That's not all you want."

"No, what I really want is to strip you, lift you up on that counter, and put myself in you as hard and deep as I can go. I'm ready, but that might be moving a little fast for you. I thought I'd start by touching you before I tasted you—your mouth, your throat, your breasts. I remember how sensitive your nipples are, Jacy."

She looked shocked. Scared. And hungry.

"Don't tell me you don't want me to," he said, and stepped in close, looking down. He could see the lace of her bra and the hard little buttons of her nipples beneath the thin cloth of her shirt.

She shook her head. "What I feel—it's only physical. Hormones. They make a pregnant woman feel…sexy. But it isn't enough."

No, it wasn't. He wanted more, yet… If he could get her to accept him again physically, surely he could get her to accept all of him, eventually.

"I can't." She held her head high, but her eyes were dark and jittery. "Don't push me on this."

For one long moment he thought he was going to do just that—touch her, hold her, overwhelm her with her own needs as he'd done once before. But he remembered the contents of his briefcase.

No. No, he couldn't do it, not now, not when he planned to push her, hard, about something else tonight. He stepped back.

He could wait…a little longer.

Jacy's knees were still unsteady when they sat down to supper, but at least she had a table between her and Tom now.

Why had he stopped? That question stuck in her head stubbornly. If he'd pushed, he could have had her. They both knew it. So why had he stopped? Was he being decent, respecting her wishes? Given their past history, she had trouble believing that. Tom had used her before. Why would he hesitate to do so again?

Maybe he just didn't want her that badly.

He asked for the bread. She passed it to him and finished getting her breath under control before she spoke. "We're giving a party."

"We are?" He sounded mildly curious as he sampled the soup. If the hunger still roiling her system lingered in his, she couldn't see it. "Why?"

"I'm not sure," she muttered, blowing gently on a spoonful of soup. "I mean, I called Nan this morning to ask who she'd gotten to move her stuff last year, and before I knew it, she's inviting people to our 'moving party.'"

He frowned. "How many people is she asking? Just because you can be up for short periods now doesn't mean you can take on anything as strenuous as planning a big party."

"Oh, I'm not doing anything. Do you think she'd let me

have anything to say or do about any of this?'' Jacy grimaced and broke off a piece of bread to dunk in her soup. "No, all I'm supposed to do is accept help graciously, she said. And get you to call her. She wants a list of—these are her words—'cops with strong backs' she can invite.''

They talked about the move and the party while they ate. It was a relief, an enormous relief, to Jacy, having something sensible and relatively impersonal to discuss. For the first time since Nan grabbed control of Jacy's moving plans, Jacy was glad for her friend's bossiness.

She was almost relaxed when they finished. Tom insisted she go lie down while he did the dishes, and since she was about at the end of one of her three-hour "up" periods, she agreed.

Instead of heading for the kitchen, though, he retrieved his briefcase. "I've got something for you.''

"Oh?'' Jacy realized she wanted it to be a present, and felt foolish. Tom wasn't the sort of man to give casual gifts, and any other sort was bound to have strings attached.

But it might be something for the baby.

He took a few sheets of paper out of the briefcase, closed it and held out the pages.

Curious, she took them. "Names,'' she said, scanning the pages. "Women's names.'' The list was divided into several groups, each group headed by the name of a different area hospital. She glanced at him, puzzled. "Are you trying in some weird way to come up with a name for the baby?''

"Those are the names of women who delivered a healthy female baby on June first in Houston thirty-one years ago.''

June first. Her birthday. Understanding hit Jacy like a blow to the stomach. *Her mother's name was on that list.* "You had no right,'' she whispered.

"You've never looked. Never tried to find out.''

"How does that make this right?'' She threw the pages at him. They fluttered ineffectually to the floor. "Didn't the fact that I've never tried to learn anything about her tell you anything? How dare you?''

"Why?" he said, suddenly fierce. He knelt on the floor beside her. "Why haven't you looked, Jacy? What are you afraid of?"

He caught her hands and held them both tightly in his. "Even now, when it might help the doctor to know your background, you haven't wanted to find out. Why? What are you hiding from?"

A tremor shook her. She couldn't hide it. "Her," she said, and her voice shook. She hated it, but couldn't get it to quit. "I don't want to know about her. She didn't want me. Why should I want to know anything about the woman who abandoned me?"

Slowly his hands loosened their grip without letting go completely. "You don't give second chances, do you?" he asked. His voice sounded odd. Almost bitter. "What about what the doctor said, Jacy? About the DES and how hard your mother must have fought to bring you into life?"

"I don't know," she whispered. It changed things. She didn't want it to. She'd fought not to look at what the knowledge altered—because as soon as she did, she felt the old emptiness yawning inside, the terrible empty place that had always been there, always.

She shivered and didn't notice it was her hands now that held on to his. "I never wanted...a lot of kids who've been abandoned or given up for adoption make up dreams about who their parents were, how they were famous or rich, how they didn't really want to give up their baby. I did that when I was really small, but pretty soon I figured out..."

"What did you figure out?"

"Look at me. Thirty-one years ago it was hard enough to raise a child born out of wedlock. How much harder to raise one of mixed blood?" She managed to shrug. "Maybe she had good reasons for what she did, but when you get right down to it, she gave me up because anything else was too much trouble." Her mother hadn't wanted her *enough*. That's what it all came down to.

"You don't know that." He stroked his hand slowly down her hair. It was incredibly soothing, that single caress. "Maybe the uncertainty is what keeps you from putting it to rest. Maybe if you knew, one way or the other, you could put it behind you."

Most of the time she thought she had put it behind her. Most of the time. "I don't know," she repeated. Challengingly she added, "Even if I did find out who my mother was, it's not likely I could learn anything about my father."

"True," he said. "They probably weren't married, after all. But if you found her, and she was still alive, you might ask her."

The idea was so enormous, and came at her so unexpectedly, she forgot to breathe. Her father...she'd thought about her mother sometimes, years ago. She'd done her dreaming when she was little; she'd set the dreams aside with some bitterness as she grew older. She'd thought she'd even gotten past most of the bitterness.

She'd never even let herself dream about her father.

He stood. "You know," he went on as casually as if he hadn't just stopped her heart, "you need something to do. If you decide you do want to go after your mother's identity, you might want to write it up. Do a series of articles or something."

She shook her head, but it was too late. The words had been spoken. The idea of finding who her mother was—and maybe her father—fell into the empty place inside her, and lodged. "Aren't you going to tell me I should do this for the baby?"

He shook his head. "Between me, you and Dr. Robbins, our baby is going to be fine. No, if you decide to hunt for your mother, do it for yourself."

Three days later, Jacy called Tabor and proposed a series of articles for the Sunday "Family" section on adopted and abandoned children who chose, as adults, to find their birth mothers.

Four days after Jacy talked to Tabor, both the new and the old apartment were full of people carrying heavy objects from one unit to the other. Jacy had managed to get almost everything boxed up herself in the last few days, but she hadn't actually transported so much as a throw pillow. She'd barely been allowed to walk from one place to the other.

She was propped up now on her red couch for her "hour off," watching as four strong men maneuvered a large dining room table through the front door of her new apartment.

The table was Tom's. Hers was going into storage. "It's incredible," she murmured.

"Aren't they, though," Nan said appreciatively. "Who would have thought Perkins from Marketing would look so good in shorts?"

Jacy gave her an amused glance. "I meant it's incredible that you coerced so many people into giving up a Tuesday evening to move my junk around."

"Oh, that." Nan flipped her hand negligently. "I don't even know half these people. Your sweetie just gave me some names to call, and I did. Everyone wanted to help. All they needed was the encouragement of a little free beer."

"Not to mention free food. Cops and reporters love free food," Jacy said dryly, glancing at the tiny patio out back, where two men were grilling hamburgers and hot dogs for the crowd on two barbecues. One was a reporter from a rival paper whom Jacy had dated briefly and remained friendly with.

The other was Tom's father.

Jonathan Rasmussin was a big man, not quite as tall as Tom but broader through the chest and shoulders, with hair the sandy brown color of his younger son's. Raz would probably look a lot like that in another thirty years. But Jonathan's eyes were like Tom's—pale like his, yes, but even more, they were a cop's eyes.

They were also a father's eyes, and something in the way they'd studied her when she met Jonathan at a family dinner three nights ago told Jacy he was going to be a problem.

Jacy didn't want to deal with problems tonight. Her emotions had been on a roller coaster for too long. Tonight she wanted some time out, time to play.

"Don't call Tom my 'sweetie,'" she told Nan firmly. "It sounds nauseating."

Nan grinned unrepentantly. "Should I go back to calling him 'that sorry SOB'? "

"Not yet."

"How about 'that lover of yours with the world-class buns'?"

"Not accurate." The damnable thing was that Jacy heard the regret in her voice herself. Her lips thinned.

"Oh?" Nan's expressive eyebrows shot up. "He does have a great butt, so you must not—"

"Down, girl, or I won't introduce you to the guy you've been ogling—the one in the ratty T-shirt." Raz was one of the men carrying Tom's big dining room table down the entry hall at that moment, and Nan's eyes tracked him the way a cat tracks the flight of a bird.

Raz called out a question about where the table went, and Nan jumped up. Jacy had shown her where things should go earlier, and she'd been bossing the men around enthusiastically.

"Have fun, General," Jacy told her.

Nan grinned. "I'm practising for when I have minions of my own." She hurried over to supervise.

For a moment Jacy was alone, but pleasantly so, surrounded by busy, noisy people. She smiled. She'd missed this—the clamor, the confusion, the crowding.

It was kind of like at Saint Mary's Childrens' Home, wasn't it?

Funny, but she hadn't realized until now how closely she'd duplicated the conditions at the orphanage in her working life. She'd always been conscious of a need for private space, since that had been a rare commodity when she was growing up, but she hadn't known she also needed the noise and confusion of having people around.

"You look pleased with yourself," someone said.

She turned her head and saw Tabor approaching from the kitchen. "You know, it never occurred to me until I started trying to write in the middle of all sorts of peace and quiet how much I hate the stuff."

He smiled. "You managed to turn out a good story in spite of all that nasty peace and quiet. Prather saw it, too," he said, referring to the editor in chief. "He liked it. It'll be in next Sunday's edition."

Jacy's breath whooshed out in relief. She hadn't wanted to admit it, but she'd been anxious about the piece she'd turned in to Tabor yesterday, the first in her "A Search for Roots" series. It was different from anything she'd attempted before. Longer, more personal. Painfully so, in places.

"So," Tabor said, curious as ever, "how goes the mother hunt?"

She shrugged. "Slowly." To begin the articles, Jacy had contacted a support organization for adoptees. She'd interviewed three people who had completed their own searches—or had given up. On her private hunt, she'd begun contacting the hospitals on Tom's list, checking the medical records of the babies born to those women.

Of course, there was no guarantee her mother was on that list. The woman might not have given birth to her in Houston, or at a hospital.

None of the babies from the list had been named Jacinta Caitlin. Tom had helped her determine that much, and it shook her. Jacy had always thought her name was the one thing she knew came from her mother because of the note. Who other than a mother—and a very young, naive mother—would leave a baby in a basket on the steps of an orphanage, with a note pinned to the blanket? The act seemed to have been lifted from a nineteenth-century novel.

Maybe, Jacy acknowledged, she just wasn't willing to give up believing that her name, at least, had come to her from her mother, but she had to organize her hunt in some fashion. She'd decided to first check out those babies who hadn't been named before leaving the hospital. Her mother might have named her after taking her home, after all.

The front door opened, spilling three of Tom's cop friends into the room—three loud, laughing, complaining men carrying the chairs to the dining table. Tom was with them. His eyes met hers. As quickly as that, her heartbeat picked up. Colors sharpened, but sounds faded as she looked into his eyes—and quickly looked away.

How was she going to keep from making a fool of herself over this man a second time?

Tom saw the way Jacy's eyes skittered away from his. He set his jaw and endured the tightening of the tension he'd lived with for far too long.

She wouldn't even look at him anymore. Was it because of what had happened—or almost happened—in the kitchen last week? Or because he'd manipulated her into looking for her mother?

Her old apartment was almost empty. Tom collected a few "volunteers" to bring the last of the things over. His brother wasn't one of them, though. Tom noticed that, just as he noticed the way Raz sat beside Jacy on the couch, obviously comfortable with her. Just as he'd noticed how often his brother had been to see him since he'd moved in with Jacy...and how often he'd dropped by to check on Jacy when Tom wasn't there.

Tom didn't look at Jacy when he left.

Seven

"**Y**ou've lost your mind," Jonathan Rasmussin said flatly.

Tom signaled the turn and pulled into the apartment parking lot. It was late. The partygoers had eaten singed hot dogs and hamburgers, drunk beer and soft drinks and gone home. Only family remained, helping get the last few things moved over, doing a bit of unpacking while Jacy kept her feet up.

Tom's father had arranged for the two of them to ride back from Tom's old apartment together. He'd used the time to grill his son. Tom had been expecting the interrogation ever since he'd introduced Jacy to Jonathan three nights ago.

Not that Jonathan Rasmussin had been rude or unpleasant to Jacy. But it had been obvious—to his son, at least—that he wasn't happy with events. "Just say what you mean," Tom said. "Quit beating around the bush."

"Dammit, Tom, this isn't a joke. You've asked this young woman to marry you."

"Yes." Tom pulled into his parking place near the streetlight. His hands flexed briefly on the steering wheel as satisfaction surged through him. He was making progress. He and Jacy now lived in *their* apartment, not hers. His things were mingled with hers, and his name was next to hers on the lease. "You want to remember that," he told his father mildly as he turned off the ignition and pocketed the keys. "She's going to be my wife."

His father snorted. "Not according to her."

They both climbed out of the Jeep. Tom went around to the back and began unloading the boxed odds and ends they'd brought over.

"I'd like a cigar," Jonathan said. "Walk with me while I smoke one?"

Tom considered picking up a box, carrying it inside and so cutting this conversation short. But his father would just find a way to have the discussion later. Better get it over with, he decided.

Jonathan pulled out one of the fat cigars Lydia Rasmussin hated. "Can't understand what all the fuss is about smoking," he grumbled as he held a match to the tip. "I don't dare light one of these things up anymore unless I'm outside, and pretty soon they'll be banning that, too."

It was a familiar complaint. "And if they do, I'll probably wind up giving you a citation since you're too blasted stubborn to give up your cigars."

"You would, too, wouldn't you?" Jonathan grinned suddenly. So did Tom. The resemblance between the two men jumped into focus as clearly as if a switch had been turned. It was a wolf's grin they shared—friendly, but hardly safe.

Jonathan Rasmussin was grayer, shorter and huskier than his oldest son. He had retired from the force two years ago but was still every inch a cop, and button-popping proud that his sons had chosen to go into the force.

"So," Jonathan said, slapping Tom on the back. "Let's walk, and I'll explain why you're an idiot."

Tom gave his father a wry glance, and fell into step with him.

The night was warm and damp, as if the heat and exertion of the day had made the air itself sweat. In the misty air the streetlights were ringed with hazy rainbows. Jonathan stepped over the low hedge that separated the parking lot from the sidewalk. Tom followed suit.

The street was better lit to the right, where a fast-food place held down the corner, trailing a string of small businesses: a cleaner's, a tarot reader, a locksmith. To the left lay a couple of older homes, and darkness. Without speaking, the two of them turned left and proceeded at a slow stroll, looking not at each other, but out at the night.

Between them, they had sixty-five years of watching the night.

"Now, I don't want you to take this wrong," Jonathan said, puffing away at his cigar as they passed out of the circle of light from the streetlight. "But the plain fact is, a woman like that is trouble. I don't think she means to be," he added judiciously. "Been watching her tonight. She draws men like honey draws flies, but she probably can't help it, the way she looks."

"I'm trying not to take that the wrong way," Tom said. "Do you really think I'll have a problem with it if my wife is attractive to other men?"

Jonathan glanced at him shrewdly. "Even if one of those other men is your brother?"

Tom recognized interrogation techniques when he ran across them. Get the subject rattled, emotional, and see what shakes loose. "I wondered if you'd noticed," he said after a moment. "It's not going to be a problem."

"Even if she resists the temptation to stir up trouble between you, it might put a strain—"

"Hold it." Tom stopped walking. They were well away from the streetlight now, and his father was a vague shape in the dark, punctuated by the glowing orange tip of his cigar. "It won't be a problem because there's no way in hell Jacy would encourage Raz, even if he did take leave of his senses. Which he won't."

The cigar's tip flared brightly as his father inhaled. "That's right," he said. "Raz won't. But the way you were watching the two of them tonight, I wasn't sure you knew that."

"I know it," Tom said shortly. Women liked Raz, always had. Jacy was apparently no exception. And Raz obviously liked Jacy right back, which shouldn't have been a problem—wouldn't have been one, he admitted, if things had been smoother between him and Jacy.

"Good," Jonathan said. "Your brother has a bad case of 'white knight syndrome,' you know. I expect that's part of her appeal for him. No real harm in it."

"You'd know about that," Tom said dryly. His father, his brother and the cousin who'd been raised with them all shared a tendency to play hero, with or without lance, steed and armor. An unhealthy trait, in Tom's opinion. He was convinced it had passed him by.

Jonathan nodded, then stood there, silently smoking. Waiting.

Tom was familiar with this trick, too. His father had used it on him often enough in the past. Be quiet long enough and the subject tends to jump in to fill the silence.

Unfortunately, knowing the trick wasn't the same as being proof against it.

An old pickup rattled down the road, followed by a white sedan. In the hush that followed Tom gave in and spoke of what was bothering him. "I expected Mom to have a problem with all this," he said quietly, "not you. Yet she's accepted Jacy and the situation better than you have."

"That's because she thinks you're going to marry the girl."

"I am."

"Why?"

Tom glanced at him, startled. "Aren't you the man who had a little talk with me when I turned fifteen? Something about either keeping my pants zipped, using protection or buying a ring, because if I got some girl in trouble her daddy wouldn't need to come after me with a shotgun. You'd do that yourself."

"What's right at fifteen and what's right at forty aren't always the same."

Restless, Tom started back toward the light near the Jeep. "If you're trying to make me believe you want me to turn my back on Jacy, don't bother."

"Well, now," his father said, falling into step with him. "If you refused to be responsible for your baby or the woman carrying it, I guess I'd still hang you up by the balls. But you've done the right thing. You've offered marriage and been turned down. I respect her for that, by the way."

Tom kept his silence, grimly certain his father wouldn't.

He was right. "You're bent on marrying her, and it's wrong. It's not fair to either of you. I don't know what her feelings are, but I know you. You don't love her."

With an act of will Tom kept his fists from clenching. "You're over the line."

"Not yet," Jonathan said as they approached the Jeep. "But I suppose I'm going to be." The tip of his cigar glowed again as he inhaled. "You want to know why I'm convinced you don't love her? First, I can't believe you wouldn't have mentioned her if she'd meant much to you before you knocked her up."

"Be careful," Tom said. "Be very careful what you say."

"You going to tell me you two *did* have an ongoing relationship, then? You'd been dating for a while?"

"I'm going to tell you it's none of your damned business."

"The real kicker is the timing." Jonathan stopped by the

hedge in front of the Jeep. "My God, Tom, do you think I can't do the math? The baby is due on March third, right?"

Tom said nothing because there was nothing, absolutely nothing, he could say.

"It was conceived about the second week of June, then."

"Leave it alone," Tom rasped. "For God's sake, drop it."

"I can't." Jonathan tossed the burning stub of his cigar away. It arced out into the street. He faced his son. "Tell me I'm wrong, Tom. Tell me you didn't take Jacy to bed after making another of your miserable pilgrimages to the cemetery. Tell me you didn't get that woman pregnant on the anniversary of Allison's death."

The knowledge of his guilt made Tom sick. It had been making him sick ever since that night. At the time, he hadn't been able to sort out which of the two women he'd wronged the worst, his dead wife or the new lover who was so very much alive. He hadn't known how to walk away from the one, so he'd walked out on the other—or tried to.

He swallowed bile and turned away, toward the apartments...and Jacy.

She stood at the edge of the light, her face bone-white in the dimness. "Is that true, Tom? Is what he said true?"

"Jacy—"

"No." Her hand slashed the air. "I don't want to hear anything else, not now. Just tell me if it's true."

"Ma'am," Jonathan said, "I'm sorry. I didn't know you were there. I would never have brought it up like that if I'd known."

Jacy couldn't move. Not yet. Nothing was working right, nothing but her voice. That was steady enough, when nothing else was. Her eyes flicked to the older man. He seemed genuinely distressed. "Don't worry about it. Sooner or later I'd have learned the significance of the date." If she'd looked at the clippings about Allison Rasmussin's death more closely, for example. The date of the issue showed in the slugline at the top of every page of the paper. Noticing that would have spared her tonight's hard lesson.

But she seldom learned anything the easy way, did she? With this man in particular, it seemed, none of the lessons came easily.

She looked at Tom again. "Tom?"

He said nothing, and damned himself with his silence.

Her breath jerked painfully in her chest. "I came out to see what was keeping you so long. You'd better come in before your mother starts worrying." She turned and walked away—carefully, because she couldn't feel her feet properly.

It was rather like being drunk, she thought as she went back inside. Like being drunk and trying desperately to act sober. She thought she did all right with Tom's mother and brother as they and Jonathan took their leave, but Tabor knew her too well. He studied her face, frowning, when she said good-night to him and Camille.

Nan left soon after that, and she and Tom were alone.

Jacy walked into their roomy new living room and looked around...at her two couches, and his dining table. Her bookcases, his desk. Her Monet prints, his mantel clock.

Her baby. Conceived on the anniversary of his wife's death.

"I'm sorry," he said from behind her.

"It doesn't matter."

"That's one of the most stupid things I've ever heard you say."

She felt the tight twist of anger, warm when the rest of her was cold. She wanted to protect that warmth, keep it close, private. "Why would it matter? I already knew you used me that night. You were so damned deliberate about it all. This just supplies your motive. I've often wondered about that."

Silence—followed by a sudden, splintering crash. She whirled around, her hand at her throat.

Tom stood near the blue couch. Shards of a white ceramic lamp lay on the table, the floor, and the couch, scattered as if someone had hit it with a bat. But Tom hadn't used a bat. Blood welled from his fist and dripped slowly onto the beige carpet. "Don't say it doesn't matter," he said fiercely.

"You're bleeding," she said, staring stupidly at the blood, shiny crimson blood, coating his knuckles and dripping, dripping.

"Don't you dare shut down on me." He started toward her.

She looked from his closed, bloody fist to his face. His jaw was tight and his eyes were wild and she wondered—she did wonder—why she wasn't afraid. "You cut your hand when you hit your lamp," she told him as if he might not have noticed. She didn't understand. Tom—orderly, controlled Tom—had punched out his lamp?

"I lost it." He stopped in front of her and dragged his undamaged hand across his hair. "Can you understand that? I'm human. Push me far enough and I get stupid."

"What are you so angry about?" she demanded. "If anyone has a right to be angry, it's me!"

"So get mad!" He put both hands on her shoulders, the clean one and the bloody one, and gave her a little shake. "Yell at me. Curse me. Tell me how sorry I am!"

She brought her hands up together then shoved them apart, knocking his hands off. "Don't touch me! Don't you ever touch me again."

"Why not?" he growled, moving in close. "Why not, Jacy, when you like it so much?"

Something cracked open inside her. "You used me! Damn you, we were friends and you used me! I knew it, I knew it from the moment you walked out the door that night. You got what you wanted and you left, but now…now—'' Her fisted hands dug her nails into her palms and she tried—she tried hard—to hold back the next words, but they poured out. "Were you thinking of *her?* When you made love to me, were you thinking of her?"

"When I touch you, Jacy, I can't think of anything but touching you more."

She drew in a shaky breath. That was something. Not much, but something.

He reached out. She backed away. "No. No touching. You owe me some answers, Tom."

He nodded, his eyes wary.

She swallowed. "What your father said…about that night. Did you go to the cemetery first, before meeting me?" The thought made her sick to her stomach.

"No." His answer came swiftly, definitely. "I'd gone there before on that date, but not this time. This time…I wanted to put the grief behind. I wanted to move on."

"Was I supposed to help with that?" she asked bitterly. "A little sex with a willing woman on the anniversary of your wife's death to convince yourself you'd 'moved on'?"

"You want me to tell you how it happened? I don't know, dammit! I'd worked so blasted hard not to let the lust and the guilt control me. For two years I'd see you and I'd want you, and it ate at me. It was like an acid, the wanting, eating away down inside me somewhere—maybe I thought I could get you *out* if I just once satisfied this craving. If so, I was wrong. I was sure as hell wrong, and I couldn't handle it."

Blood pounded in Jacy's ears, an angry drumming. "So you walked out on me."

"Yes. I'm not proud of it, but that's what I did."

She wanted to scream, to rage at him, hit him…hurt him. Instead, she heard herself speak the one truth she'd fought to keep hidden. "You hurt me," she said. Her voice broke. "I thought I knew you, and you hurt me."

"I'm sorry," he said again, and for once his emotions

were easy to see in his eyes—winter eyes, haunted by his own pain and the knowledge of hers.

"What is it you want? My forgiveness?"

"Can you give it?"

"I don't know." She shook her head, dizzy with emotion. How could she forgive him? How could he even ask her to? "I don't know *how*."

When he spoke again, some quality in his voice chilled her, warned her. "There's one more thing I should tell you about that night. I didn't want you to know any of this, but maybe I was wrong about that. Maybe you have to know it all."

"What?" What more could there be?

"When that driver smashed into Allison's car, she was two months pregnant. I didn't know until she went into surgery. She may not have known, either."

She stared at him. Her anger drained out, as if his words had created a vacuum. And in that vacuum was only one thought at first: Tom's baby died. Along with his wife, he'd lost his baby.

Two months pregnant, she thought then. Jacy had been two months and four days pregnant when she went to police headquarters and told him he would be a father. A few days later she had nearly lost their baby. She looked at him now, standing braced and blank-faced in front of her, and realized he expected her to be angry about this, too.

How could he think she would be angry? Unless—maybe that's what he wanted from her, anger and blame. Maybe, in the irrational way of humans, he felt guilt over a death—two deaths—he was in no way responsible for.

Something nameless and complex moved inside her, a feeling as bitter as winter and as irresistible as the coming of spring. It had nothing to do with pity, and everything to do with need.

His need or hers? She didn't know. For the moment, just this one moment, it didn't matter. Whatever the force filling her, it steadied her as she moved closer to him. She didn't know what to say, so she lifted his damaged hand and cradled it in both of hers.

Jacy intended, vaguely, to give comfort. Whatever effect the contact had on him, the result for her was like closing a circuit. The thrill sang in her blood like an electric charge, exciting and excessive. She kept her head down, swallowed, and tried not to cry. "I'm sorry you lost your baby, Tom."

"I didn't want it," he said, his voice terrible with grief and guilt. "I'd told Allison I didn't want to have children. I was afraid to. I'd seen so much…"

Now she looked up. The bleakness on his face made her lose the battle, and tears blurred her vision. "You wanted the baby," she said softly. "Maybe you were afraid, and maybe you didn't know about it until it was too late, but you wanted it."

He said her name. His hands came up to her face, and her tears spilled over. He cupped her cheeks and jaw, and his thumbs stroked the dampness from her cheeks as if she were the one who needed comfort.

Maybe she was.

"Jacy?" he said again.

She turned her face in his hands and kissed his palm.

He stood very still for a long moment. Then his eyelids lowered as he looked at her mouth. He bent.

His lips were soft against hers. Whatever his intent—taking or giving comfort, gratitude, the simple need for contact—the mild intimacy stirred the singing in her blood. Irresistibly her lips followed his when he withdrew.

His need or hers? She was afraid this time she knew the answer.

His mouth came back to her. His lips were more definite this time, stating his sensual intent clearly and wordlessly. His hands slid from her cheeks to her jaw, her throat, down to her shoulders. She shivered. He pulled her against him, and she went gladly. If she worried for a moment about his hand and the untended hurt, she forgot everything else in the sheer joy of tasting him again.

His body was hard, perfect. At this point, even his clothes felt perfect—crisp cotton, rugged denim. The textures delighted her, offering just enough of a barrier to heighten the tension. Her fingertips slipped inside the collar of his shirt to tease the nape of his neck. He shuddered and deepened the kiss.

That quickly, delight changed to hunger.

Heat flowed through her, basic and urgent. Jacy moaned and pressed against him. His hands raced over her, testing, molding, inciting. She wanted this—yes, this hunger, the splendid burn of passion— *I can do this,* she told herself. *I can have what I need. I'm not expecting anything this time. I won't be hurt again.*

"Jacy," he said, tearing his mouth away to press kisses across her cheek. "I'll stop if you ask me to. I swear, this time I'll stop if you tell me no."

She looped her arms around his neck. "Don't stop."

"Thank God," he said, so heartfelt and sincere that she amazed herself by laughing. She was still laughing when he swung her up into his arms.

It felt sweet, giddy, frightening. "Tom?" She clung to him. "You aren't going to try climbing those stairs carrying me, are you? I'm no Scarlett. I don't need a lot of romantic trappings."

"Maybe I do. But just this once," he said, turning toward the longest couch, the red one, "I'll compromise."

On the inside, Jacy was laughing again as he lowered her and followed her down—but only inside, because her mouth was busy with his.

Yes, she wanted this, needed it. She didn't need Tom, she told herself as her fingers fumbled with his buttons, hungry for the feel of his skin. But she needed the heat, the speed, the sheer dazzlement of her senses he could bring her. *Release,* she thought as she pressed kisses across the chest she'd exposed. *That's what I need—the huge, dizzy plunge, and the release.*

She willfully ignored the fact that she only wanted it from one man. This man.

"Jacy," he said as her hands on his chest, her lips on his throat, drove him up hard and quick. "Sweetheart, give me a minute. Slow down."

She couldn't slow down. She didn't have a minute. If she got him inside her—once she got him inside her—everything would be all right again. She knew that. Breathless, needy, she pulled his shirt out of his pants. "I want you in me, Tom. Now."

He groaned and pushed her dress up past her waist. His hands were hot against the skin of her stomach, her thighs. Then they raced up her body to her breasts. He cupped them, kneaded them, while his mouth came back to hers, and his tongue plunged inside.

The kiss went on and on. Jacy had been wild before. She was crazy now, ready to demand that he hurry. Or to beg. Her hands went to his waist, and she fought with the snap of his jeans and then the zipper.

He was large and throbbing beneath the placket. She made a frustrated noise when she couldn't get the zipper down, and stroked her hand along him. He hissed, and pushed her hands away. Then he tore his mouth and body from hers, and stood.

"All right," he said. "We'll do it your way. You want it fast? Take them off," he told her. "Take your panties off. I want to look at you."

Jacy wiggled out of the lacy triangle while he pulled off his boots and tossed aside his shirt. His eyes never left her.

Then he paused, his hand on his zipper. Her dress was rucked up to just beneath her breasts and she was bare from the waist down, and he just stood there looking. The longer he stared at her, the hotter she got, until she was breathing through her mouth in soft, quick gasps.

It was enormously erotic, lying there exposed, watching him strip while he looked at her, his eyes hot and acquisitive. He was lean and muscular and, in places, he was scarred—and he was *hers*. For now, for this joining, at least, he was hers.

She opened her arms to him as well as her legs as he came down on top of her for one more kiss. Their mouths were already joined when he raised her hips in his two big hands and slid into her. Slowly. Carefully. Completely.

She cried out, in wonder and in need. With slow, patient strokes, he answered her cry. But she couldn't stand patience from him, not now. With her teeth and nails and the urgent thrusts of her own body, she demanded more, harder, faster.

Again he answered. If he held anything back, any part of himself that stayed behind on their mad race to watch and be sure he didn't hurt her or the baby, she was too lost in the oblivion of speed to notice.

They moved together, each glorying in the freedom of needs, long suppressed, that they now set loose—needs that were both met and doubled with each plunge, each sweaty movement of bodies locked in the sweetest of rhythms.

He stabbed the fingers of one hand through her hair and took her mouth with his. She gave him her tongue and claimed his in return, fierce and rejoicing as she raced straight at the cliff's edge. A moment later her body bucked against his when she hit the white-hot, endless space of climax.

She cried out, and didn't know it was his name she called.

He followed her over.

Tom managed to collapse onto his side instead of directly on top of her, though with the narrowness of the couch, they stayed almost as close together as they had been a few seconds ago. Her legs tangled with his. His arm pillowed her head, and he felt the heat of her breath on his shoulder. She lay snuggled up to him.

In the quiet aftermath, Tom could hear his ragged breathing, and hers. He waited, hoping against hope she would speak to him this time as she had the other time they were together. Then, she'd spoken softly to him of delight and discovery. She'd made him smile. Damn her, she'd cracked something inside him open that night, something he'd been trying ever since to wall up tight again, but it was too late.

It had been too late then, but he hadn't realized it in time.

When she'd seen his smile on that other night, she'd turned unexpectedly playful. She'd started tickling him—which had led inevitably to a second lovemaking.

But Jacy wasn't going to talk or play this time, was she?

Tom lay there in silence, holding the woman he'd wanted for so long…a woman who didn't give second chances. The longer he lay there, the more certain he became.

Having her physically wasn't enough. Compared to what he'd had and tossed away, this wasn't nearly enough.

Eight

Jacy had never woken beside a man before. She suffered no moment of disorientation or surprise the next morning, though. Before her eyes opened she knew where she was, and who had crowded her to the very edge of the bed. She remembered making love the first time downstairs on the couch, and the second time, long after supper, here in Tom's bed.

This is nice, she decided drowsily, pleased with the heat of his body, the cool comfort of cotton sheets...the novelty of not being alone in the first moments of the day.

Tom was as greedy asleep as he was awake, she decided with a sleepy smile. He sprawled over the biggest part of the bed. One of his legs lay alongside hers, and his arm was flung over her waist as if he were claiming her. *Or maybe,* she thought, amused, *he's just staking his claim to the small corner of the bed he's left me.*

But it was nice, very nice, to lie there and watch her

lover in the hazy predawn light. She could let herself enjoy this closeness as long as she didn't expect it to last.

The light had shifted from near-dark to gray when she saw Tom open his eyes. He looked at her and smiled as if he were happy to wake beside her.

Alarm stirred, but it came from so deep inside she could almost ignore it.

His hand left her waist to cover her breast. "Good morning," he said, his voice thick with sleep, his thumb gently rubbing her nipple. And all at once she was awake, wide awake, with zippy little flashes of heat rocking through her system.

I can do this, she told herself as she smiled back and her flesh came alive beneath his slow stroking. *I can have him without needing him.*

"They're more sensitive now, aren't they?" He looked pleased with himself. A bit smug. He tugged the sheet down then and smiled at the sight of her breasts. After a moment his expression changed. "It won't be all that long before our baby is nursing there, will it?"

An ache moved through her. It swam up from a place too deep inside, too private, a place no one should have been able to reach—an ache that had nothing to do with sexual hunger. The feeling was rich and necessary, like taking a full breath after years of constricted breathing, and it terrified her.

He isn't going to stay, she reminded herself. She couldn't need him, not in any way except the thoroughly physical one in which they'd joined last night. So she cupped the hand that touched her breast, pressing it more firmly to her.

"At the moment," she said, "it's just you and me in this bed, and you're giving me some interesting ideas about how to start the day." She smiled, threaded her fingers through his hair and urged him closer. "How about a good-morning kiss?"

She thought he was going to turn her down. For one

second he looked like a cop, not a lover—skeptical, knowing. Panic touched her. She couldn't afford for him to know what she felt—what she had *almost* allowed herself to feel. He'd use it, just as he had used her before.

Then he bent to her breast and kissed her good-morning that way, and soon enough she forgot her reasons for offering herself in the delight of having her offer accepted. And it was safe, perfectly safe, to allow herself this pleasure, because her feelings for Tom hadn't changed at all after making love to him again.

By noon, the sun had burned off the last of the clouds that had been drizzling rain on Houston the past couple of days. When Tom pulled into Resthaven Cemetery at 1:15 that afternoon, the sky was a hot, hazy blue. Grass rolled over the acres of graves in waves of green as gaudy as a parrot's feathers.

He'd spent the morning interviewing witnesses in a celebrated murder case Special Investigations had recently inherited from Homicide—celebrated because the suspects all came from two prestigious families. The rich, Tom had discovered long ago, had pretty much the same problems the rest of the world did. Chances were good the murder had been committed for very traditional reasons: either love or money.

Tom was putting his money on love this time. Of course, some people would argue that an emotion so twisted with jealousy that it drives a lover to kill her beloved isn't really love.

After twenty years on the force, Tom didn't agree. Love came in all sorts of shapes and forms. Some were prettier than others, less confusing. Less elemental. He'd been reminded of that today when he tried to crack the alibi of a young woman who had probably killed her older lover rather than continue sharing him with his wife.

That's why he was at Resthaven today—because there was more than one way for a man to love a woman.

Tom parked his Jeep in one of the lots scattered around the grounds and picked up the bouquet that lay on the seat beside him. It was a modest handful of flowers he'd bought at a florist's along the way here because it had daisies in it.

Allison had loved daisies.

In a world of straight lines and right angles, the shapes here at the cemetery were different. Paths wound around the grounds in curves, bending here, dipping there; plantings were scattered, not locked behind straight lines or in square beds. The graves themselves were gently rounded mounds.

The path he walked now was bleached gravel, unreasonably white in the afternoon sunshine. It crunched beneath his feet, a vaguely satisfying sound that blended pleasantly with the occasional song of a bird. The noise and haste of Houston faded here, cushioned by the trees surrounding the place…and, perhaps, by something timeless and immaterial that rested here, along with the dead.

He paused by an elm that looked as if it had stood vigil there for a hundred years. That tree was the main reason for the spot he'd chosen to lay her to rest. He'd wanted her to have the shade and the birdsong.

He set his palm against the trunk of the tree. His eyes closed for a moment.

She wasn't here. He knew that. Whatever mysteries death concealed, Tom knew Allison was gone from this world. Yet love isn't logical. Whenever he came here he stopped by the elm and placed a hand on its trunk, glad it was here for her.

When he reached her grave he went down on one knee to lay the bouquet in the grass. He was supposed to get the groundskeeper to provide a vase and water for the flowers, but he never did. He wanted them to rest right on top of the earth that covered her, and if the flowers faded and died a bit more quickly this way, what did that matter? Allison, too, was dead.

"Hi," he said softly. The ground was damp. He felt it through the denim of his jeans. "I'm not sure why I'm here today. I guess...do you know about Jacy? If you do, then you probably know more about why I'm here than I do."

She'd often understood what he felt before he did. Tom fell silent, remembering. Allison and he had grown up together, so he had a lot of memories to call on. They'd drifted apart as young adults, then come back together years later as if they'd planned it that way.

She hadn't been perfect. Not a perfect woman, or the perfect wife for a policeman. He was beginning to understand that she'd been too dependent in some ways, fearful about his job and so oblivious of mechanical matters that she'd run her car out of gas every two or three months and called him at work to come get her.

She'd also been gentle and funny and loyal, and incredibly dear. "You were so easy to love," he told her. "I was the hard case. Isn't that what you used to tell me? That I was a hard man to love, but worth it? Well," he said unevenly, "I've found another hard case, and I...dammit, I never expected to care again. I don't know how to handle it."

For several minutes he knelt there in silence. A bird called from nearby. Another answered. His pant leg grew damp from the ground beneath him.

Tom didn't receive absolution, or feel the comfort of his old love's presence one last time. He didn't imagine her whispering her blessings to him. Mostly he felt quiet and private and alone as he knelt there, and yet...not entirely alone.

When he stood, he stared at the flowers he'd brought her for a moment longer. He smiled then, but it was a sad smile, because he understood some things he hadn't before. Guilt, like grief, can become a way to hold on to someone who's gone.

Sometimes, the answer was as simple, and as sad, as saying goodbye.

When Tom walked in the front door at eight o'clock that night, Jacy was pacing the living room.

"I should have called," he said automatically, setting his hat on the small table in the entry. He had to set what he carried on the table, too, so he could take off his jacket and begin unbuckling his shoulder harness. "Sorry I'm late."

"What?" She stopped, looked at him, and shook her head. "Oh. No problem." Belatedly she added, "I hope you didn't have a bad day?"

And that, he thought, amused, ought to teach him about making assumptions. Jacy's mind was obviously occupied by more important things than whether he was on time for supper. He hung his shoulder harness next to his jacket. "Not bad, but frustrating. I was trying to track down a lead and kept hitting dead ends." He picked up what he'd set on the table a moment ago.

"I know how that feels," she muttered, adding, "There's some Moo Shoo Chicken in the refrigerator if you're—what's that?"

"Flowers," he said. "I think they're called 'bird of paradise.'" He walked over to her and held out the elegantly exotic stalks wrapped in green florist's paper.

"I don't need flowers." But she took them from him quickly and held them up to her face.

"There's not much scent, I'm afraid."

"No," she agreed, staring at the flamboyant orange blooms, her expression soft and surprised. "But they're beautiful."

"They reminded me of you."

Now she looked up. Wariness warred with the pleasure

on her face. "I would have pegged you for a roses man. These are...different."

"You don't like them?"

She didn't look at him. After a moment she shrugged. "What's not to like? They're spectacular. I'd better get them in water." She hurried into the kitchen.

Tom followed, wondering what he'd done wrong. Were the flowers too showy, and she didn't like that? Had she wanted the traditional roses? Or was she still so uncertain of him that anything vaguely tender or emotional made her pull up the drawbridge?

He thought about their lovemaking that morning. Jacy accepted one sort of emotion from him now, but she might be using their mutual passion to block out other, more dangerous feelings. "So why were you pacing when I got here, if you weren't upset over me being late?"

She knelt beside the one unpacked box in the kitchen, rummaging through dish towels and miscellany until she came up with a tall, green vase. "I'm a little edgy, I guess."

"Something wrong?"

"No." She went to the sink to run water into the vase.

Both his eyebrows went up. "Well, that's good." He went to the refrigerator and took out the little white boxes from the Chinese place a few blocks away. He grabbed a beer to go with it, turned around and dangled the bait. "I'd ask if it was that time of the month, but it can't be, can it?"

She rose to it beautifully. Eyes blazing, she rounded on him. "Oh, if that isn't just like a man! As if everything in a woman's life is tied to her hormonal clock!"

He smiled. "So," he said gently, "if it isn't your hormones tying you up in knots, Jacy, what is it?"

She just looked at him for a moment. The water filled the vase in the sink behind her, then overflowed. She turned around and shut it off. She took her time pouring out the excess water, then fussed with the way the tall stalks sat in the vase.

Finally she spoke. "I learned my mother's name today."

"Jacy." He crossed to her quickly and set his hands on her shoulders. She was stiff, resistant. He didn't care. He turned her to face him. "That's big news."

Her eyes shone, but it was an angry sort of pain he saw, not happiness. "Annabel. Annabel Margaret Mulhoney. What kind of a name is that, Annabel Margaret?" She pulled away and started to pace.

Tom didn't know what to say. "How did you find her? Was she one of the women who took her baby home before naming it?"

"The Mulhoney baby left the hospital still unnamed, but I don't know who took it home. The records mention a birthmark on the left hip, like mine. And there's the foot-prints." Thirty-one years ago the nuns had needed to es-tablish an official identity for an infant whose origin was unknown. It hadn't been simple. Among other things, they had footprinted their new charge. Jacy had a copy of that record to compare with the newborns' footprints in hospital records. "It's not definite, of course. I'm no expert at matching footprints."

But it must be pretty certain, to have her wound up this way. "So you looked at her record," he said carefully. "What did you learn?"

She stopped and looked at him, but the woman who made her living putting things into words apparently couldn't speak of this. She turned and headed to the living room.

Tom followed.

"See for yourself," she said, taking a large envelope from the folder where she kept her search materials. "I've got a copy of her record. You look."

He took it from her and pulled a blurry photocopy out of the envelope. There was little enough to read. On June first, thirty-one years ago, Annabel Margaret Mulhoney had been delivered of a baby girl. Then she'd hemorrhaged, and died.

"I'm sorry," he said quietly.

Jacy stood near the patio door, staring off into some private distance. Her arms hugged her waist. Her voice was tight with anger. "She was only nineteen years old, Tom. She was only nineteen years old when she died."

Tom had to guess, and hope he guessed right. Jacy's anger might be born of fear. Her mother had bled to death in childbirth. It would be only human for Jacy to be afraid now that she faced the same ordeal. Or her anger could be part of the enormous disappointment of learning her mother's identity, only to discover that it was forever too late to get to know the woman.

Or her anger might be rooted in guilt. Tom chose instinctively. "It wasn't your fault, Jacy."

"Wasn't it?" She swung around, her arms wide. "I've blamed her. All these years I've blamed her, only she *died*. She took medicine to help her give me a chance to be born, and then she died giving birth to me and I—I— Do you know what I thought when I was little?"

"Tell me."

Unable to be still another second, she paced a few jerky steps before she stopped, one hand resting on her stomach. She rubbed it as if she were trying to soothe the tiny life growing inside her, to protect it from the wildness of her own emotions. "Did you ever wonder why I wasn't adopted? Babies, even mixed-breed babies, could usually find a home. Not me. She didn't relinquish her rights to me, you see. No, she—or someone—just dumped me on the steps of St. Mary's like an unwanted kitten. It was years before the court would formally terminate my unknown mother's parental rights. Courts were very careful of parents' rights in those days," she finished bitterly.

"If you feel guilty for thinking it was your mother's

fault, you shouldn't. Someone had made it impossible for you to be given a real home. What was more natural than to think it was your mother—even to hate her for it?''

"But I didn't hate her," she whispered. "Not for a long time. Not until the day when I turned seven and something one of the older girls said—well, you might say she gave me a reality check. Until then...I knew why the courts wouldn't let me be adopted, you see. There was a chance she would come back for me. And...for a long time, I believed she would.''

Oh, God. Tom could imagine it all too easily. Jacy at five or six had probably been all hair and bones and scratched-up skin from a dozen scraps or tumbles. The green eyes and dusky skin would have made her look exotic even then. Different. It was hard on a child to be different.

And so she'd told herself tales. Tales about the mother who had given her into the care of the nuns but would return someday, and then she would have the family she craved.

Tom would have gone to her then. He wanted to, badly, but some instinct honed from years of asking questions and listening for the answers, spoken and unspoken, held him still. Jacy wasn't finished.

After a moment, she sighed and looked at him. "All these years," she said. "All these years, I've been sure my mother must have been the different one, the one from Mexico or Italy or wherever. Look at the name she gave me. Only it wasn't her, was it? Now I find out her name was Mulhoney." She smiled, but it was a wretched effort. "What kind of a name is that for an Italian, Annabel Margaret Mulhoney?''

She was so bright and brave and stubborn. She wasn't going to come to him, wasn't going to admit to either of them she needed comfort.

But when he went to her and put his arms around her, she leaned against him. *It's a start,* he thought as he slowly

combed his fingers through her hair. "I imagine that thinking of her as being different, the way you felt you were
different, made you feel a little closer to her."

She gripped the sleeve of his shirt in one hand and laid
her cheek against his chest. "So," she whispered. "What
do I do now? Do I keep looking? I had a father. Annabel
must have had relatives. Do I look for him, for them?"

"Only you can answer that, Jacy. If you decide you want
to look, I'll help. Either by helping you search, or by staying out of your way, if that's what you want."

She was silent for so long he gave up on getting an
answer and just stood there, running his fingers through the
wild curls that trailed past her shoulders. For once she was
willing to let him hold her when they weren't having sex,
and he was guiltily aware of how much pleasure that gave
him.

Tom didn't dare push her this time. He didn't know exactly what Jacy needed, or how she could find it. He knew
what he wanted, though. If she could find a way to forgive
the first, most terrible abandonment, maybe she could come
to forgive him, too.

"Someone dumped me on St. Mary's steps two months
after Annabel died," she said at last. "I want to know who
it was, and why. Do you think we can find out anything
after so much time has passed?"

"Oh, yes." He grinned with a hunter's disciplined ela-
tion. "If there's any kind of trail, I'd bet on us to find it.
After all, I'm a damned good cop—and you aren't so bad
at what you do, either."

He knew the muffled sound she made was a chuckle
when she punched him in the stomach.

For the next week, Jacy attacked her new search with
the single-mindedness that had made her a top reporter, but
this investigation was different. This time she *had* to know.
She'd spent most of her life persuading herself that who

she came from was unimportant compared to what she did with her life. She still believed that was true professionally.

But on a personal level...on a personal level she was lost. Maybe it was the new life she carried that created her obsession with the past.

Or maybe it was Tom, and what he made her feel both in bed and out of it. She tried not to think about that.

She had a name. That was the center of their search, her mother's name, because the hospital records were incomplete. Nothing on them indicated who had taken the tiny baby home. For the next eight days, though, that name didn't seem to do them much good.

Oh, they got a little more information. It only took two days for Tom to get confirmation of the footprint ID from an FBI expert who owed him a favor, so they knew for certain that this woman, this Annabel Mulhoney, had truly been her mother.

By checking with the funeral homes nearest the hospital, Jacy learned who had paid to have her mother's body readied for burial: Eagan Mulhoney, Annabel's father. But they found no Eagan Mulhoney in area phone books or property tax rolls. Nor did the man have a Texas driver's license or vehicle registration.

The garage apartment where Annabel had lived before going to the hospital had been torn down fifteen years ago, and her former landlord was dead. Tom had walked the block, looking for older residents who might remember her, without luck. A contact at the electric company confirmed that Eagan Mulhoney had lived in Houston, and that he'd worked at a service station. But he'd discontinued electric service right after his daughter's death, and they didn't have a forwarding address.

According to hospital records, Annabel had gone to a free medical clinic during her pregnancy, but it had been a shoestring operation that folded in 1970. So far they hadn't tracked down anyone who had worked there, but Tom was following up a lead on one of the nurses.

On Thursday, Jacy turned into her parking space at the apartment after running a few unavoidable errands. She turned off the ignition and sighed. She did know a little more than she had eight days ago, she told herself. She knew that Annabel hadn't lived with her father, though she had been young and unmarried and, as far as they could tell, unemployed. They didn't know whether she'd been living on her own, with a roommate, or, just possibly, with Jacy's unknown father...the one who was different, like her.

Eagan Mulhoney had apparently left town right after his daughter's death. He hadn't waited around long enough to take his new granddaughter home from the hospital. So she also knew he hadn't wanted her. He wasn't the one who had named her and left her on the orphanage steps.

Jacy was distracted as she climbed out of the Mustang, carrying a department store shopping bag. She was halfway to the apartment when someone said her name. She jumped.

"I hope I haven't come at a bad time."

She turned to find Jonathan Rasmussin watching her. His expression was so like Tom's it reinforced the thoughts of character and heredity that had preoccupied her lately. "No," she said a bit warily. She hadn't seen Tom's father since the night of the party, though Lydia had kept in touch. "You've got pretty good timing, actually. I've got another forty minutes of 'up' time—long enough to put some coffee on, if you'd like to come in and have a cup."

"Thank you. I'd like that."

"It's decaf," she warned as she started for the front door.

"My doctor would be pleased. You're feeling well, Jacy? My wife tells me you're very faithful to the regimen the doctor has you on."

"No problems, aside from a tendency I've recently developed to doze off whenever I stop moving for long. Lydia and my books agree that's normal for this stage.''

The occasional drowsiness wasn't the only recent change. Three of the purchases in the shopping bag she carried were bras in a larger size, but she didn't care to mention that to Tom's father.

They talked about unimportant things while Jacy got the coffee started. Once they both had a mug, though, Jonathan spoke with a bluntness that again reminded her of his son. "Jacy, I told you on the night of the party how sorry I am for what you overheard. I wanted to do something to make it up to you for whatever hurt I caused, so...I hope you don't mind. Tom has told me some of the details of your search, and I took it on myself to do a little digging.''

Her heart pounded with a mixture of alarm and anticipation. "What do you mean?''

He set his mug down. "I had an idea. It was a long shot, but I wondered if the Mulhoneys might have been immigrants. The names are distinctively Irish. 'Eagan,' in particular, isn't uncommon in Ireland, but is almost unheard of here. I have a few contacts still, and—well, to make a long story short, I tracked Eagan Mulhoney to California through his visitor's permit. He became a naturalized citizen there.''

He took a deep breath. "I found your grandfather, Jacy. Eagan Mulhoney is still alive.''

Nine

"**I** need to go to Beaumont tomorrow," she told Tom at supper that night.

"What?" He set down his fork and frowned. "You know I have to be in court. I don't think you should drive there by yourself."

Jacy toyed with the noodles on her plate. Normally this was one of her favorite meals. The tomato-basil sauce and the angel-hair pasta were both freshly made—not by her, of course, but the deli at the grocery store did a great job. "I checked with the doctor. He said a short car trip should be okay." She'd called soon after Jonathan left.

"You want to tell me what's going on?"

She might, if she could just figure it out herself. That's why she needed to go to Beaumont. "Your father came by today."

His expression softened. "He told me he might."

"What else did he tell you? Did he say why he was

coming over?'' His expression made her exclaim, ''Don't tell me he asked your permission!''

''He was raised to protect women, Jacy. He's not going to change at this date because his ideas about a man's role don't suit your ideas of independence.''

Her lips thinned. ''I suppose you think I should be glad you gave him *permission*.''

''I told him it wasn't my decision to make.''

Jacy struggled to get her temper under control. It wasn't Tom she wanted to strike out at. It wasn't really Jonathan, either. ''So what did he tell you?''

''He's tracked down Eagan Mulhoney, and he was afraid his news about the man would be upsetting. He didn't offer any details, and I didn't ask for them. But he did mention that Mulhoney is in California—not Beaumont, Texas.''

''He didn't say where in California?''

Tom shook his head.

''He's in Evansville Prison.'' Saying the words gave her no relief. She still felt jumpy, on edge—as if she could dodge the truth by reacting quickly enough.

Tom exhaled sharply. ''That's rough, sweetheart.''

Sweetheart. He called her that in bed sometimes. How odd to hear it at the supper table.

''Did he say what Mulhoney is in for?''

She noticed that Tom didn't refer to Eagan Mulhoney as her grandfather, the way Jonathan had. She was trying her damnedest not to think of him that way herself. ''Murder.''

The word created a moment of silence. She shrugged as carelessly as she could. ''Second degree. Your dad says he's got a record, though, so he's been locked up a long time. Apparently he gets drunk and gets mean. He got into one bar fight too many, hit someone a few times too many. Beat the poor guy to death. Damn,'' she said suddenly. ''I wish I'd never started this.'' She shoved back from the table, grabbed her plate and headed for the kitchen.

She went to the sink and started washing the pan she'd

cooked the pasta in. Tom came up behind her and laid his hands on her shoulders. He felt warm, solid, seductively real behind her. "Are you really sorry you started looking?"

"I don't know. No," she said, and shut off the water. "It has to be better to know the truth." Jacy had lived by that creed too long to abandon it now, even if she couldn't quite believe it at the moment.

She set the pan on the counter and thought about turning around, into Tom's arms. But she was too jittery, too angry...too needy. She moved away to wipe down the stove.

"I hate thinking I'm related to someone like that. God only knows what I inherited from him." A tendency toward cruelty or alcoholism? She scrubbed the stovetop viciously.

"There's no reason to think you inherited anything from him except those green eyes of yours."

"Maybe." But Jacy didn't believe that. She didn't think Tom's father did, either. He'd referred to Mulhoney several times as Jacy's grandfather, proving how conscious he was of the blood tie between her and the man in a California prison. "And maybe I can guess why Annabel wasn't living with her father back then. He probably hit her."

"He didn't have an arrest record here. He may not have turned violent until he lost his daughter. Grief...can change a man." Tom came up behind her again and began kneading her shoulders.

His massage brought warmth, but not comfort. No, the way he made her feel wasn't comfortable at all. Each gentle flex of his fingers added another layer of heat and memory.

They slept together now. Jacy, who had never woken with a man before, slept in this man's bed every night, and he touched her in bed with those strong fingers. The heat pooled in her belly and curled lower. She shivered.

No. She couldn't stand to want him. Not now. Jacy pulled away again and tossed the sponge into the sink. "Maybe he was just roughing up his daughter back then, and didn't graduate to hitting strangers in bars for another few years.''

He didn't speak. After a moment his silence drew her reluctant eyes to him. "You can stop running away," he said grimly. "I was trying to help you relax, not seduce you. Though I suppose you could accept the seduction better than—'' He broke off, ran a hand over his hair.

"I didn't…I—oh—'' Because, of course, she *had* been running. In circles, since it wasn't really him she was trying to get away from. "I'm trying," she said helplessly. "Sometimes I just don't want to be touched." Except that she did. The contradictions churning inside her were too much for her. How could she explain them to him?

He wore his closed, cop's face. "So what do you want, Jacy?''

His question wiped her mind blank. She had no idea.

He smiled unpleasantly. "I'm talking about the investigation. Do you want to keep looking?''

"I don't know." She spread her hands wide. "I know less than I ever have in my life, it seems. But…" In the midst of confusion, one need swam into focus. "It wasn't him. Eagan Mulhoney wasn't the one who named me. He left before I had a name. Oh, it doesn't make sense, but I have to know who named me!''

"All right. We'll keep looking, then. If Mulhoney will cooperate, he's the quickest route to the answers you need. I'll get a private detective to talk to him, since this isn't—''

"That's expensive." She shook her head. "I don't think I can afford it.''

"I can." He scowled.

She scowled back. "I thought your finances were limited.''

"A couple of days on a private detective's tab is hardly the same as paying for two households for several months. Besides, I've got a contact in San Diego who owes me a favor." He switched subjects quickly. "Now what does all of this have to do with going to Beaumont this weekend?"

Nothing. Everything. She rubbed her arms, but it didn't help. Her chill was on the inside. "I need to see Sister Mary Elizabeth." Visiting Sister Mary Elizabeth would help. Jacy knew that. She'd put it off too long, afraid the sister would be disappointed in her, but no more.

She had to get her bearings. Talking to the nun would be like finding firm ground to plant her feet on so she could look around and figure out where she was.

Tom looked blank. "Who is Sister Mary Elizabeth?"

"From the orphanage. She…" How to explain? Jacy settled for giving the bare facts. "She was one of the caretakers at St. Mary's. She's eighty-four now, and lives in a church-run nursing home. She had a stroke three years ago. I get over to see her at least once a month, and I'm late for my visit."

"Every month?" He looked at her oddly. "You see her every month? She must be important to you."

There was something odd about Tom's voice, something that made her own heart squeeze uncomfortably. "She's special."

He waited, as if he wanted her to go on. Jacy didn't want to. He was in so many parts of her life already—in her memories, in her bed, even in her thoughts when they weren't together. She had to keep something separate. Some place inside her where he'd never been.

When she didn't speak, he did. "You'll have to call her instead of going in person," he said brusquely. "You don't have any business being on the highway in your condition. I forbid it."

She stared. "I can't believe you said that."

"Believe it. I don't want you on the highway."

She tried to make allowances. His wife and unborn child had been killed in a vehicle accident, after all—though it had happened in city traffic, not on the highway. "The weather should be clear, and I'm a good driver. Check my record, if you don't believe me." He didn't smile. She tried again, holding on to her temper with both fists. "Beaumont's barely an hour and a half away, Tom."

"And an hour and a half back."

"I can stay overnight if it will—"

"You're not listening. I don't want you going. Don't try to go against my wishes in this, Jacy. I'm warning you. If you do, I only have to make one phone call. You'll be pulled over before you've gone twenty miles."

"This is ridiculous," she snapped. "I've got the doctor's permission. I don't need yours."

"I know damned well you don't *want* to need anything from me. You don't want to need anyone at all, do you?"

"I'm certainly not going to rely on a man who starts threatening me when he doesn't get his way—a man who's already walked out on me once."

"And you're not about to forget that, are you? Any time I get the least bit close outside of bed, you drag that hurt out of whatever closet you keep it in and wrap yourself up in the pain all over again."

"I don't have to keep reminding myself of what a jerk you can be. You're doing a fine job of reminding me yourself right now!"

"But you don't mind if I get close in bed, do you, Jacy?" His voice dropped, and he moved right in front of her. "I can get plenty damned close there, can't I? As long as I'm quick about it. As long as I make sure you get in a good climax or two—"

She slapped him.

He stared at her long enough for self-disgust to join the other emotions roiling through her. She'd hit Tom twice now. Was she like her grandfather?

He turned and headed for the front door, grabbing his hat on the way.

"Where are you going?" As soon as the words were out she hated herself for needing to ask.

"Out," he said, and tugged the hat on his head before slamming the door behind him.

Tom called his brother from his car. Thirty minutes later they were at a lighted basketball court at a school near Raz's apartment. An hour later, dusk had come and gone, and they were both winded and dripping.

Raz tried to block Tom's shot, missed and nearly fell on his face. He leaned forward, his hands on his thighs, and concentrated on breathing. He was going to have to give up smoking. Soon. "Okay," he said, still huffing as he watched Tom make the basket. "You dragged me out here for a reason, I'm sure. Have you finished humiliating me for now? Can we talk about this?"

Tom moved restlessly, dribbling the ball from one hand to the other. "You've been hanging around women too much, brother, if you want to start talking things out."

"I like women." With an effort, Raz straightened. "Maybe that's what's bothering you." Raz had noticed the way Tom had kept an eye on him and Jacy at the party last week. Until then it hadn't occurred to him that his brother could doubt him in that way. The idea pinched more than a bit.

Tom shot him a disgusted look along with the basketball. "Idiot. Here, see if you can make a basket if I promise not to distract you."

Raz caught the ball, relieved by the insult. "Then we must be here to punish you, not me."

Tom snorted.

Raz dribbled the ball as he circled the basket, moving easily in spite of his complaints. "No? Then you're just in a bad mood, and decided to take it out on me." He took his time, then made his shot. "I would have thought that having sex regularly would mellow you out more."

The ball sailed gracefully through the hoop. His other shot landed on target, too.

"How old are you now—nineteen or twenty?" Tom growled. "Mentally, I mean, since physically you're dragging around like an old man. You still think all problems between a man and a woman can be fixed in bed?"

"Maybe not, but a man can have a hell of a time trying." He dribbled out to the free-throw line, crouched. "You gonna tell me what's wrong, or shall we go back to killing each other over who gets to make the ball go through the little hoop?" The ball sailed out and up—and bounced off the rim.

Tom moved and reached, recovering the rebound with a quick grace a man of his mature years had no right to, in his younger brother's opinion. "We already know who can make the most baskets." He didn't put the ball back into play this time, but passed it back and forth between his two big hands. After a moment he said flatly, "Jacy wants to go to Beaumont."

This didn't sound earthshaking. Raz waited.

"I didn't want her to go. I forbade it."

Raz groaned.

"Then I told her that if she went anyway I'd have her picked up by the DPS."

Raz looked at him incredulously. "You *what?*" He shook his head. "I can't believe it. My by-the-book brother threatened to use his authority to hassle a civilian for personal reasons?"

Tom shifted his feet. "I wouldn't have actually done it."

"Ah. So you weren't abusing your badge—you were *lying* about abusing your badge."

"Dammit, Raz, I—" He stopped, ran a hand over his hair. "Yeah, I was lying. She just makes me so crazy. Do you know why she wants to go to Beaumont?"

Raz waited again.

"She wants to go visit a nun who's in a nursing home

there. Seems this Sister Mary Elizabeth helped raise her. Jacy goes there once a month. Once every damned month. And she's never mentioned the woman. Not even before we—not even back when we were friends. I didn't know Sister Mary Elizabeth existed.''

Raz heard the hurt. It went deep, deeper than he'd realized. After a moment he said softly, "So she doesn't tell you everything. Do you tell her everything? Does she, for example, know you're in love with her?''

Somewhere nearby, a mother called for Jimmy to come in "right this minute." A dog barked. A car pulled out of a driveway and started down the quiet street.

Tom stood motionless in the glare of the court's artificial light. Finally he said simply, "No, she doesn't. There's not much point in my telling her right now, either. The time to say those words came and went a few months ago. Just like I did.''

Raz knew more than their parents did about the circumstances surrounding Jacy's pregnancy, having been on the spot the day Jacy slapped those paternity papers on Tom's desk. He'd caught Tom at a weak moment, and wrested part of the story from him—so he knew what Tom was talking about. "Women need the words.''

Tom gave him a disgusted look. "I know what women need. But she won't believe me now. And if she did—if she did, I think she'd run as fast and far as she could. I just don't know *why,* not exactly. It has to do with her growing up in that orphanage.''

"Then maybe you need to talk to someone who knew her then,'' Raz said softly. "Someone like this Sister Mary Elizabeth.''

The Sisters of Mercy Nursing Home was housed in an unlovely, U-shaped building that rested in a shallow valley a few miles outside Beaumont. It was operated by Sister

Mary Elizabeth's order, but the residents were drawn from all walks of life.

Jacy still wasn't sure how Tom had persuaded her to put her trip off until Saturday so he could come with her. It certainly wasn't because he'd come crawling back, begging her forgiveness. In Jacy's wildest fantasies she couldn't imagine this man begging for anything.

No, Tom had walked in a little after ten Thursday night and informed her he was a fool to try to forbid her anything since that guaranteed that she'd do it, no matter how damnfool her idea was. He'd added that his stupidity was the direct result of hers, since she'd gotten him too worked up to think straight—and that he would take her himself on Saturday.

As apologies went, that one stank. And yet, that's exactly how things had worked out. The strangest thing was that Jacy didn't feel she'd been bludgeoned or manipulated into agreeing. It was almost as if part of her did want him here, and that made no sense at all.

So they drove to Beaumont together on Saturday. Jacy wore the bright red top and tropical skirt she'd worn for her first visit to the doctor's office, for similar reasons—to give her courage, and because the sister, who never wore colors, loved to see her in red. They took Tom's Jeep, but listened to Jacy's music. The Beach Boys, Elvis and the Supremes filled the Jeep with sound and song—which was just as well, because Jacy and Tom were barely talking to each other.

They'd slept together after he'd come home Thursday, but sleep was all they'd done. Both Thursday and Friday nights Tom had turned his back to her when he got in bed, and he'd slept on his own side without crowding her at all.

Jacy didn't know if he was still angry, if he was trying to teach her some obscure lesson—or if his desire was simply dying a natural death after nearly two weeks of having her pretty much whenever he wanted to.

They were barely speaking when they arrived at the nursing home at 10:10 that sunny September morning. Inside, the building was plain to the point of near poverty, but somehow the purely functional took on an austere beauty rather like that of an old, well-scrubbed kitchen table.

"Sister Mary is in the courtyard," the matron at the front desk, a lay employee, told Jacy. "You know the way, sugar."

The closer Jacy and Tom got to the exit to the courtyard, the less she was aware of the tension between them as another sort of tension gripped her. Jacy didn't understand it. She never felt nervous about visiting Sister Mary Elizabeth, but today her palms were damp. She wiped them on her skirt.

Tom glanced at her. "Relax," he said in a softer voice than he'd used with her in two days. "I promise not to pick my teeth or swear in front of the sister."

"I didn't think you would," she said, feeling unreasonable and irritated.

"No?" He lifted his brows. "It occurred to me you might be feeling a bit like a daughter bringing a suitor home for the first time. You might even be wondering if Sister Mary Elizabeth will approve of me."

"Don't be ridiculous," she said, looking straight ahead and resisting the urge to wipe her palms again. "Sister Mary Elizabeth isn't some kind of mother figure for me. For heaven's sake, she's a *nun*."

"I think I grasped that part," he said.

The courtyard was a surprise to most visitors, for here austerity departed. A row of cherry laurels screened the open end of the courtyard, which was shaded by sumac and ash as well as its walls, and planted with everything from ferns to flowers. The sister in charge of the grounds was a passionate gardener who made the most of a muggy climate where the temperature hovered between uncomfortably warm and too blasted hot most of the time. Plants loved the combination.

So did some people. Seldom, Jacy thought with a smile as she started across the flagstone portion of the courtyard, did the weather get too hot for Sister Mary Elizabeth. The nun's love of heat had been the basis for a lot of teasing over the years.

Only a few residents were enjoying the courtyard that morning. One tiny, erect figure in a wheelchair sat alone in the northwest corner of the courtyard, her ancient face lifted to the sun, waiting. The sight of the old-fashioned wimple and habit eased the tightness across Jacy's shoulders.

At that moment Sister Mary Elizabeth turned her head and saw Jacy. She smiled, and Jacy's nerves evaporated in a rush of familiarity and love. That smile was a bit crooked these days, the less-responsive muscles on one side a legacy of the stroke, but it glowed as brightly as ever.

"Sister," Jacy said, and went to her and knelt to take one fragile hand in hers. It was like holding air wrapped in soft, thin chamois cloth.

The old woman's face folded into a million lines as her smile deepened. "You are well," she said. "I can tell. Worried, but well—but you can tell me what worries you later. You wore my favorite color for me, didn't you, Jacinta?"

Tom held back a few steps. He thought Jacy needed this moment of reunion to herself. He didn't know why she insisted Sister Mary Elizabeth wasn't a mother figure, when the love shining in her eyes said otherwise. Maybe that was part of what he'd come here to learn.

The sister's appearance was a surprise. From the religious names the woman had taken, Tom had been expecting an Anglo, but Sister Mary Elizabeth looked like pure hidalgo Mexican. He thought she must once have been very beautiful. Now she was as wrinkled as a raisin, and frail.

The two women exchanged words and pats and smiles

for a minute before Jacy stood and motioned Tom forward. "This is Tom Rasmussin, Sister. He's a detective with the Houston police, and a friend."

Tom stepped forward. The old woman tilted her face up and smiled at him. Her dark eyes were lightly filmed with cataracts, yet they stirred no pity for infirmity in him. It was like seeing smooth, water-polished stones through the distortion of a rushing stream—he knew the stones were there, solid and real, even if all he saw was a wavering image. He smiled back.

"So you have brought a young man to meet me at last," Sister Mary Elizabeth said in a voice slightly slurred by the effects of her stroke.

Jacy protested that Tom was neither young nor hers. Tom brought a couple of chairs over from a nearby table, and Jacy sat automatically, laughing when the sister teased her in her slow, slightly impaired voice about protesting too much. Tom took the other chair.

"No, no, you have always loved the truth too much to lie well, Jacinta," Sister Mary Elizabeth said. "You and this man are not 'just friends.'" She turned her head to study Tom. "Are you?"

"No, ma'am." Something in the glowing serenity on that old face struck a familiar chord with Tom, yet he was sure he'd never seen the woman before. "It must have been a great help to you if she's always been this poor a liar. I imagine you had your hands full enough with her as it was."

She laughed a dry, nearly soundless laugh. "Oh, yes," she said. "Always so curious. And stubborn. She did not like to take anyone's word for anything, did you, Jacinta? And if a rule did not make sense to her, she ignored it. Like with the puppy." The old eyes filmed over even more now, with memories. "Do you remember the puppy, Jacinta?"

Tom listened while the two women reminisced. It

seemed that Jacy had found a puppy one day and smuggled it to her room, where she bribed or blackmailed the girls who shared the room with her into silence about their new roommate. Unfortunately, she'd been unable to keep the puppy itself silent, and had to give it up a couple days after finding it.

It was, said the sister with a hint of sadness, one of the few times Jacinta even tried to lie to her. But she had wanted that puppy very much.

Tom lost track of the conversation as they wandered on to other memories. He kept thinking of a little girl who always told the truth trying to lie to a woman she loved—because she wanted a puppy so badly.

Had she needed something of her own to love? Something that loved her back—just her, not her and a couple dozen other, equally needy charges?

Tom waited until the conversation lapsed briefly. "I hope you ladies will excuse me a few minutes," he said, standing. "One of the tires seemed a little low. I'd like to check the pressure before we head back." He'd promised to give Jacy some private time. She couldn't very well discuss him while he was there, after all.

He was rewarded by the first genuine smile Jacy had given him in days.

Tom grimaced as he walked away. It seemed typical of the state of their relationship that he pleased her best with his absence.

"Sister," Jacy said as soon as Tom moved away, "there's something I have to tell you."

Jacy had confessed many failings to this woman over the years, but telling Sister Mary Elizabeth that she was pregnant and unwed was one of the hardest things she'd ever done. Deep down, Jacy had always been conscious of having been someone's *mistake*. She didn't want anyone, not even Sister Mary Elizabeth, thinking her baby was a mistake.

Sister Mary Elizabeth wanted her to marry Tom. In some ways the nun was remarkably modern; she'd wanted all her charges to be able to support themselves, to have careers if they wished. But as far as children and marriage went, her ideas were straight out of the last century.

"I was foolish once," Jacy told her. "I convinced myself he was…someone else. That doesn't mean I should be foolish for a lifetime."

"But you are living with him."

In explanation, Jacy told the sister about nearly losing the baby and why Tom had moved in. She talked about her search for her mother's identity—and what she'd learned about her grandfather. "Remember what you said once?" she finished wistfully. "Jackie had been teasing me about not knowing who my parents were. You said that whoever I came from must have had a great store of good inside them, since they gave the world me." She shook her head. "You weren't often wrong."

"We all have a store of good inside us," the sister said. "Some people make bad choices, and the good withers. Perhaps your grandfather is such a one."

Murder was a bad choice, all right, Jacy thought. "A lot of the things passed from parent to child aren't choices—everything from learning disabilities to depression and schizophrenia."

"Which makes you singularly blessed, for you have none of these problems."

Jacy smiled in spite of herself. "I suppose you think I should be counting my blessings instead of worrying over what I can't change, but I—I don't feel like I know myself anymore."

"Because of this grandfather in prison?"

"That's part of it. I can't work, and that's hard. Then there's Annabel."

"Your mother."

Jacy nodded. "Even if I didn't know her, I had ideas about her. I guess they shaped the way I thought of myself more than I realized. I *forgave* her for abandoning me—and now it turns out there was nothing to forgive, that she died bringing me here." Jacy's eyes watered, and she wiped the moisture away angrily. "It changes who I am. I can't explain it any better than that. It just does."

"How could it not, to learn that someone died for you?"

Those words went through Jacy like a surgeon's knife.

Sister Mary Elizabeth smiled gently. "You have always been confused about your mother. Do you remember what happened after the puppy was taken away from you, *cara?* You were very angry. You didn't want to be there at St. Mary's. You wanted your mother to come take you away to your 'other home,' the perfect one you had made up in your mind. But that night you came to me. You couldn't sleep. You were afraid she really would come and take you away, and you didn't want to go."

Jacy had forgotten that part of the story. It was true, though—once she'd managed to convince herself her mother might really come, she'd panicked.

She reached for Sister Mary Elizabeth's hand again and squeezed—lightly, because the flesh and bone she held had grown so fragile this past year. "If you're trying to persuade me that I was just as mixed up in the past sometimes as I am now, you've succeeded."

"People do not feel only one way, Jacy. It is easy to make wrong choices, because we all feel many things at the same time. That is why it is so important to forgive."

Jacy didn't see what forgiveness had to do with it. If you made a wrong choice, the way she had when she went to bed with Tom the first time, you learned from it and went on. She'd done that, hadn't she?

Well—she *was* in Tom's bed again, but she hadn't opened her heart to him this time. She'd even gotten past the bitterness, mostly, when she learned the truth about why he'd taken her to bed that night.

Memory rose like an echo in her head. Wasn't that what she'd thought about her mother? That she'd gotten past the bitterness of being abandoned? Yet she'd been wildly disoriented ever since she learned the truth about Annabel. *Does that mean I've allowed the bitterness to coat my thinking all this time without realizing it?*

But how do I get rid of it, then?

For once, talking to Sister Mary Elizabeth hadn't helped. By the time Tom came back, Jacy was more miserably confused than ever.

Ten

Tom gave the women thirty minutes alone. When he returned, the sister was visibly tiring, though she looked content with her weariness in the way of most cats and a few fortunate old people.

They talked for a bit longer, but it was obvious the visit had drained the old woman. When Jacy suggested tactfully that she and Tom needed to be getting back, Sister Mary Elizabeth said rather fretfully, "Before you go, please see if I left my small Bible on the table by my bed. I cannot think how I came out here without it. I am accustomed to having it with me."

As soon as Jacy was out of earshot, the nun turned to Tom. "You had best speak quickly. She'll realize soon enough that I have my Bible with me, as always."

Tom was amused by the nun's maneuvering, and a bit taken aback at being read so easily. "I did want to ask you a question or two."

"You think I must be very old and wise to have seen

this?" The sister gave her dry laugh again. "I am old, certainly. But even my old eyes can see how you watch her. I trust you will persuade her soon to marry you."

"I hope to, ma'am."

"Good." When she smiled this time, Tom suddenly knew why she seemed familiar. Twice in his life he'd been fortunate enough to know people who persuaded him of the reality of the spirit—for how else could he explain the way they'd glowed more and more as their bodies aged? As if the spirit inside were burning its way out, and soon there would be nothing left. Just light, too bright and pure for this earth.

"Now," the sister said, "you have brought me comfort. I am glad Jacinta will have you, once she fights her way past her own stubbornness. What would you ask?"

"When you two were talking, you referred to something that had happened after you left. Did you leave St. Mary's before Jacy did, then?"

Sister Mary Elizabeth looked away. She lifted one thin hand to touch the crucifix that hung around her neck. "Women such as myself have long been called 'brides of Christ,'" she said at last. "Our vows bind us as permanently as marriage used to bind a man and a woman. Jacinta was fifteen when my order called me away from St. Mary's, and I obeyed. Jacinta…she had been left behind so often, you see. First, by her parents. Later by teachers, friends from the orphanage who were lost through adoption, to foster homes, or even to return to their original homes…" She shook her head sadly.

Over and over Jacy had been left. Even this woman, who had loved Jacy, had left her. Tom felt grief and panic in equal parts. "Yet she kept in touch with you. In the first shock of learning you were leaving she may have felt angry and abandoned, but she got over it. The two of you are still close." Somehow he had to do what this woman had done—get Jacy past the hurt.

Sister Mary Elizabeth's wispy eyebrows lifted in gentle surprise. "Oh, no. No, you misunderstood. The sad thing is that Jacinta was unhappy, but not terribly upset, when I went away. Part of her had expected it for some time, I think. No, what would astonish Jacy would be to find that she did believe in someone unconditionally. She wouldn't understand that, not at all."

Jacy's doctor had her scheduled for a checkup every three weeks, so she went to see him that Monday. Tom didn't go with her this time.

They hadn't made love since their argument, and the distance between them in bed was overtaking other areas of their lives. When they ate, when they talked, when they slept together, something large and unseen seemed to sit between them, keeping them from ever quite touching. An invisible giant.

Jacy shook her head as she drove to the doctor's. Pregnancy must have been making her fanciful. She even had the weird idea that the "giant" had to do with something Tom was waiting for her to say or do, which proved that her perceptions were as skewed as everything else in her life right now. Tom was a blunt man. He was used to getting his way. If he wanted something from her, he'd say so, wouldn't he?

Of course, he had held back some truths...like not telling her he'd taken her to bed that first night because he needed to blunt the grief he still felt for another woman.

She decided she didn't want to think about what he might be holding back now.

Jacy left the doctor's office at two o'clock feeling relieved and a bit dazed. He thought she was doing well under the current regimen. The baby's heartbeat was strong, and Jacy had gained three pounds. The doctor was pleased with that, too.

So was she. There was a small but definite bulge to her

belly now. She wore loose dresses in the summer anyway, so she hadn't needed to buy any maternity clothes. But she was suddenly hungry to *show,* to have people look at her and know she was carrying a child.

She drove straight to the nearest large department store.

Jacy wasn't normally much of a shopper. She'd always been so busy. But today she took great pleasure in buying a huge T-shirt that said, Baby On Board. It was royal blue with fuchsia letters. She bought a pair of maternity jeans and, for no reason whatsoever, she bought a sexy party dress with sequins and pleats that would grow right along with her. Then she went to the infants' section.

Clothes for newborns were so *tiny.* And soft. Jacy held one whisper-soft receiving blanket up to her cheek and wondered about the fragility of beings who needed such softness. Instead of bright, primary colors, she looked at pastels and pale sherbet shades, at quiet pinks and blues, yellows softer than the down on a newborn chick. She felt giddy, a little overwhelmed…and alone.

The sense of being a single in a world meant for pairs crept in on her as she overheard snatches of conversations between the other shoppers. One woman wondered if her husband would kill her if she spent forty dollars on a party dress for a ten-month-old baby. Another chatted with her friend about the twin boys her daughter-in-law had just brought home from the hospital, and how proud her son was of his sons.

The conversations all spoke to Jacy of couples—of people who continued to be part of a pair after their child was born.

Jacy was standing next to a crib piled high with blankets and stuffed animals when she suddenly understood what Tom was up to. Why he didn't make love to her. Why there was a giant "presence" between them.

She'd made him promise not to mention marriage when she agreed to let him stay, and Tom kept his promises. He wasn't reaching for her in bed because he wanted something from her he couldn't tell her about. He wanted to marry her.

Strangely, she wasn't upset. Tom's behavior was manipulative, of course. He was trying to use her desire for him to get what he wanted, and she probably ought to be angry. But she stood there stroking a downy-soft receiving blanket and hurt for him. He'd lost one child before he even knew it existed. He was afraid he wouldn't really be part of this baby's life after it was born and Jacy no longer needed him financially.

She had to reassure him. She had to find ways to let him know he wouldn't be on the outside looking in, that he would be included.

Maybe...maybe she should consider letting him continue to live with her and the baby after it was born.

When Jacy went home to put her feet up, she had a lot to think about. She slipped her sandals off, curled up on the couch and cautiously considered the future until, in spite of herself, she dozed off.

When the doorbell rang several hours later, she was wandering the apartment barefooted, muttering to herself. Tom had picked a lousy night to be late. She'd cooked, for one thing. The lasagna wasn't dried out yet, but it would get that way.

More important was the question she was trying to decide, a question that demanded discussion. She would ask, she told herself as she checked the peephole and saw Raz standing outside. Just as soon as Tom got home, she would ask him if the idea of marriage was the giant sleeping in their bed, the reason he didn't touch her anymore. And she would let him know she was thinking about letting him stay—not that she would consider marriage itself, of course, but—

"Jacy," Raz said as the door swung open. He wasn't

smiling. "I don't want to alarm you, but there's been a shooting."

Her hand flew to her throat. "Tom?" She said his name, but she didn't believe it. She couldn't think of any other reason for Raz to stand there and tell her solemnly that there had been a shooting—but not Tom, no, that wasn't possible. Tom couldn't be hurt.

But Raz didn't understand that it was impossible. He didn't say what he was supposed to say. "I don't think it's serious," he told her, "but you might want to come down to the emergency room just in case. He, uh, wasn't conscious when his backup called it in, so I don't—"

"Let's go," she said, stepping forward so he had to move back. She pulled the door closed behind her.

Raz drove. Jacy didn't try to pretend to either of them that she was fit to be behind a wheel. They took her Mustang because Raz's sports car was a two-seater and they hoped, they both hoped very hard, they would be bringing Tom back with them.

Raz couldn't tell her much more. He'd gotten word of the shooting indirectly, from another cop who'd been called by an officer on the scene. But they knew Tom had been shot in connection with a case he'd been working on, a murder case involving a couple of Houston's wealthiest families. They knew he had a head wound, and that he'd been unconscious at one point.

The hospital where he'd been taken was only twenty-five minutes away from Jacy's apartment, but it was an incredibly long twenty-five minutes. Jacy talked about the case on their way to the hospital. Talking about the case was a great deal better than thinking about Tom and head wounds.

Raz dropped her at the emergency entrance and went to park the car.

Jacy hurried inside and glanced to her right, at the waiting room. It held two sick children with their mothers, an elderly couple, three teenagers, a man in a suit and a uniformed police officer. She glanced in the other direction. The admitting clerk was chatting with the triage nurse.

She ignored them all and started for the treatment area.

"Hey!" someone called. "You can't go back there!"

That was a stupid thing to say. Obviously she *could* go back here—she'd already done so. She passed the first treatment room, which was occupied, but not by Tom. A hand grabbed her arm.

Jacy stopped and looked at the large, frowning woman in green scrubs who held her arm. "Lieutenant Tom Rasmussin," Jacy said. "Where is he?"

"Honey, only relatives are allowed back here. You'll have to wait out front."

Jacy explained very clearly, "You don't want to be putting your hands on me. I'm pregnant and I've nearly miscarried once and I'm going to see Tom now. He's been hurt. You don't want to try and stop me."

Someone down the hall called, "It's okay, Nancy."

Jacy looked past the nurse. The cop in uniform was hurrying toward them. She recognized him now. He'd been at her moving party.

The nurse insisted it was not okay, that the doctor did not need to work around hysterical family members, which proved to Jacy how little the woman's opinion was worth. Jacy was neither hysterical nor family. But the woman did drop Jacy's arm.

Then she heard Tom.

She headed for his voice. It came from treatment room five. The door was open a crack.

"...can't believe you had him call my brother, Myers," Tom was saying. "I was only out for—ouch! Watch it, would you?"

"Shut up, Lieutenant," a woman said, "and hold still so I can put a bandage on your owie."

Tom muttered something. Another man's voice—probably Myers's—said that next time Tom got himself shot he'd just leave him lying there and wouldn't call anyone at all, because he was so nice and quiet when he was unconscious.

Jacy pushed the door open.

Tom sat on an examining table. His shirt was all bloody. So was his face, though some effort had been made to clean the worst of it off. A woman in a white lab coat stood in front of him, trying to apply a second butterfly bandage to an oozing cut high on his forehead.

When Jacy stepped inside, Tom turned his head sharply, winced, and scowled at her. "Well, damn. How did you get here?"

"Shut up, Tom," she said, beaming, dizzy with relief. "And let the nice doctor put a bandage on your owie."

They didn't even keep him overnight. Jacy had a list of symptoms to be aware of, and she knew any head injury had to be watched. But he was so obviously himself, so blessedly whole. She could hardly stop smiling on the ride home.

Tom could hardly stop complaining. He'd fall silent for a few blocks, then start again. Myers had been a bloody idiot to have the desk sergeant call Raz, and Raz had been even more stupid than Myers, because he'd involved Jacy. The second time Tom started in on his brother, Raz told him to behave or he would tell their mother about his injury, too.

That kept him quiet for several blocks. "I still don't understand why you had to drag Jacy down there," he muttered as they turned onto the street the apartment was on. "You should have waited until you knew something definite."

"All right," Jacy said, turning around in her seat. Tom had insisted on riding in the back. "That's enough. What do you think Raz should have done, Tom? He knew you had a bullet wound. An ambulance took you away. Should he have waited to see if you died or not so he wouldn't worry me with anything nonfatal? Good grief,'' she said, shaking her head, ''I had no idea a little pain made you so whiny.''

He looked offended. *''Whiny?''*

''You wouldn't be this grouchy if you'd take the pain medication the doctor gave you. It's very mild.''

''I don't like pills,'' he muttered. ''They make me sleepy. If I want to turn my brain to fuzz I'll drink scotch.''

''He's just embarrassed,'' Raz said. ''He let a rookie get the drop on him.''

The shooting shouldn't have happened. Tom had gone to question a suspect, who had panicked and run. A couple of uniforms on patrol had seen Tom in pursuit and acted as backup, one staying with the car, the other joining Tom in foot pursuit. But the uniform on foot was a rookie. He had fired when he had no business even having his gun out. His shot had clipped Tom, knocking him out for a couple minutes and making him bleed like crazy.

Jacy wondered what Tom would say when he found out she'd phoned Tabor from the hospital while he'd been filling out insurance forms. She couldn't write the story herself—she was too angry, too involved. But when one cop was so trigger-happy he accidentally shot another officer, the story needed to be covered.

Tom probably wasn't going to agree with her on that score, though.

Raz came inside with them when they got home ''In case Tom keels over,'' he told Jacy cheerfully as she unlocked the door. ''Not that I'll try to catch him. I might hurt myself. But if he topples I can make sure you don't try grabbing him.''

''Thanks a lot,'' Tom muttered. ''Now go away.''

''What's that smell?'' Raz asked, sniffing.

Jacy groaned. "Burned lasagna." She'd forgotten all about it. "I'll never get the pan cleaned."

Tom looked at her. "You cooked?" Then he blinked, an odd expression on his face as his gaze drifted over her. "Jacy—"

"I'll see if any of it's salvageable," Raz said, and headed for the kitchen.

"Don't look so astonished," Jacy told Tom. "I do cook sometimes. Come on, now, you need to go upstairs and lie down."

"Jacy—"

"I think the part in the middle is still okay," Raz called. "Either of you want some?"

Jacy grinned and shook her head. As far as she could tell, Raz had no taste buds. "Help yourself." She slipped an arm around Tom's waist. "Come on, tough guy. You're going to bed."

He let her get him started up the stairs. He still had that odd look on his face, but it was mixed with amusement now. "Jacy."

"What?" He felt warm and solid and wonderfully alive next to her.

"You must have left the apartment in a hurry when Raz told you I was hurt."

"Well, yes. Of course, I've been known to burn dinner even when I'm home. Are you hungry? I don't recommend the lasagna, even if Raz thinks it's edible."

"I'm not talking about you burning supper. Look down, Jacy."

She glanced at him, puzzled, then did as he suggested. And saw...the bland beige carpet that covered the stairs, and her own bare foot on the next riser.

She'd forgotten to put her shoes on, and never even noticed.

She nagged Tom into taking one of the pain pills. He was right—they did make him sleepy. He nearly dozed off while she was helping him get undressed, and was sleeping soundly by the time she got back downstairs.

Raz ate the middle out of the burned lasagna and left. Jacy threw the rest of the meal away, pan and all, and ate a peanut-butter-and-banana sandwich while she soaked in the tub. She pulled on her softest, oldest nightshirt, brushed her teeth and checked the time—11:05.

With an hour still to go, she headed downstairs and found things to clean until midnight. Then she went upstairs and woke Tom for the first time.

His pupils were evenly dilated. He told her how many fingers she was holding up, answered her questions and went back to sleep.

Jacy would have liked to climb into bed with him, but she was afraid she'd sleep too soundly. So she went into her bedroom and set her own alarm for the first time since moving into this apartment. Then she tried to read a murder mystery.

But there were so many images jumping around in her head—some of them from what *hadn't* happened. Tom hadn't been lying pallid and near death when she reached the hospital. And when she'd stood in the doorway of the treatment room, still scared but shaking more from relief than fear, he hadn't reached out and told her how much he needed her.

When the alarm went off at 2:00 a.m., Jacy was awake and thinking of everything that hadn't happened, and wasn't likely to.

She'd left the light on in the bathroom shared by the two bedrooms. With the bathroom door slightly open, it was dim but not dark when she went to wake Tom the second time.

He sprawled dead-center in the middle of the bed, the sheet halfway up his bare chest. And she was glad, so glad to have him there, hogging the bed. She sat on the bed, scooted over next to him and touched his shoulder.

He blinked at her a couple times, then he smiled.

Her heart did a slow roll-and-thump. Fear and wonder jammed together in her throat, because for a second she thought she recognized that smile. It looked like the way he smiled at someone he—

"You don't have to hold up any fingers," he said. "I still know my name, too, what day it is, and who's president. And I know I've been very lonely in this bed. Where have you been?" His hand curved around her ankle.

Her heart tangled up with all those other feelings caught in her throat. "Your head," she managed to say.

"Doesn't hurt at all." His fingers stroked her calf now.

The honeyed warmth of desire had never felt sweeter than it did at that moment, when she smiled down into his smiling eyes. "Tom, your head can't be better this quickly."

"Everything's relative," he murmured, and tickled her lightly behind her knee. "My head is giving me a lot less trouble right now than a certain other part of my body."

She wanted him. Dear heaven, how she did want him, with an ache that started somewhere deep inside and spread all through her, slow and sticky as molasses. "Tom," she said, and bent to brush her lips lightly across his so she could savor the tingles. "We can't."

"Maybe you can't, but I damn sure can." He threaded the fingers of one hand through her hair and pulled her mouth back to his. His other hand drew her leg up over one of his.

Rich and dark, the hunger spiraled through her. She took what he offered and longed for more—more to take, more to give. The need to give to this man was as strong as the need to have him. She stroked his cheek, his jaw...and she started to tremble.

He knew. Somehow he knew it wasn't passion that shook

her now. "Sweetheart." His hand left her nape to rub along her back. "What's wrong?"

She tucked her face up against his neck where she could breathe him in. "I was afraid," she whispered. "When I heard you'd been shot, I was really afraid."

"I didn't want to upset you. That's why I was mad at Raz for telling you."

She pushed up on her elbow to frown at him. "He was right to tell me."

"Sometimes," he said softly, reaching up to trace the arch of her eyebrow with one finger, "right and wrong get a little fuzzy for me where you're concerned."

She bit her lip, suddenly frightened again—for a very different reason. Because she understood for the first time that Tom truly cared about her. *Her*, not just his duty, or their child.

He cared. And she knew it. How could she not start expecting—wanting—so much more now that she knew? How could she protect herself against the jagged edges of her own needs if there was the slightest chance he might answer those needs?

He felt her tension, but misunderstood the cause. His arm tightened around her. "I'm all right, Jacy. I promise."

"Are you sure?" She found the courage to smile into his eyes, her fingers toying with the hair over his ear. She found traces of dried blood there. "You're a mess," she said softly. "I don't want to do anything that would hurt you."

He smiled wickedly. "Well, I am a little weak. You're going to have to take it easy on me. Go slow."

Go slow? Her heart began to pound so hard she heard it like the slow throb of drums in her ears. *Go slow,* she told herself. She lowered her mouth to his again.

She teased his lips open with her tongue. The taste of him slid through her like a shot of whiskey. In that moment, he was every extreme she'd ever imagined, distilled into one sweet mouth for her to sup at. She spent quite awhile at his mouth.

He let her. One of his hands rested at her nape, the fingers kneading gently. The other slid up and down her calf. He made an approving sound deep in his chest.

Jacy had made love with Tom many times. She'd been an active lover, even demanding. But she'd never made love *to* him. This was...different.

She slid her hand down his chest. He had a wonderful chest, firm, lightly furred right in the center. She loved the way his muscles jumped at her touch. Hungry, suddenly, for other places to taste, she drifted her mouth along his stubbled jaw and down his throat. There, the strong beat of his pulse mingled with the smell that was uniquely his.

She teased his nipple with her fingertips. His breath jerked in his chest. His pulse leaped beneath her mouth.

His response triggered hers. Suddenly she was open—dreadfully, completely open to him. She seemed to feel his pleasure at her touch, pleasure as keen and needful as her own. His hunger—or hers—made her hands clutch at him in sudden demand, while their breaths turned harsh and her fear—or his?—clogged her throat.

Her mouth rejoined his, avid now as she automatically sought the oblivion of speed, the sensual battle they'd waged in the past as they chased glory together.

He groaned, kissed her back—and turned his head slightly, separating their mouths. "Slowly, sweetheart. Slowly."

A rush of feeling wiped her mind blank for a second. Meanings seeped back in slowly. Tom was injured. He was *mortal,* as this day had proved. She had to go slow...slow enough to feel...everything. She shuddered and lifted her head. "Tom?"

His eyes were two pale flames in the dimness. "It will be all right, Jacy," he said, his voice husky as he cupped her head with one of his big hands. "I promise."

When he drew her down, drew her mouth back to his, she shuddered again, and let him.

There was no race this time, no challenge. No contest. Though Tom lay on his back and Jacy lay across him, she wasn't the aggressor. Instead, she let him lead her into a new landscape, a strange, languorous place of pleasure so drugging she lost track of her reasons for being there.

His mouth was magic. His body was hers, as surely as hers belonged to him and answered to his bidding. And it was easy. She hadn't known passion could be simple, even lazy, like a summer sky flooded with blue that burned slow and hot.

When his fingers moved between her legs and teased, she slid with easy pleasure off of the first peak. When she kissed her way down his body and took him in her mouth, he moaned and moved and gave her, with his pleasure, as much joy as she'd just taken from him. And when she shifted fully on top of him, his hands digging into her hips, her hand guiding him inside her, they sighed together in a relief as vast as the clouds they drifted with.

But he didn't move. His breathing grew harsh with restraint, but he didn't move, and his clasp on her hips held her still, trapped motionless with him. He was inside her and around her, and she had the fleeting fancy that she was inside him, too—yet he didn't move. Jacy felt his urgency in his taut muscles, and she felt something else, something so complete it stopped her breath along with her thought. Then he shuddered. She moaned and ground herself against him, and the storm broke.

He thrust up. She met him. The lazy clouds they'd drifted on whipped apart in the quick winds of passion.

In the peaceful, empty hour before dawn, Tom slept. Jacy lay awake in his arms and fought to find strength.

Hadn't she reassured herself, the second time she accepted Tom into her bed, that she was safe because their passion hadn't changed her feelings for him at all?

She'd been half right. Her feelings hadn't changed...not after making love the second time. Not after he'd walked out on her, either. She'd loved him all along. But there was nothing safe about the way she felt, nothing safe anywhere in the treacherous new world he'd brought her to.

When the phone rang at 9:27 the next morning, they were both still asleep. Tom woke first and answered it. Jacy lay there and enjoyed her drowsiness.

She watched Tom's cop face slide over his features as he talked, so she assumed it was police business and didn't pay much attention—not until she heard him ask where and when the services would be held.

Alarm thudded into her then, shaking off the last traces of sleep.

When he hung up she was sitting up in bed, silently demanding answers.

"Sweetheart," he said, laying his hands on her shoulders, "I'm sorry. That was the nursing home. Sister Mary Elizabeth died in her sleep last night."

Eleven

Sister Mary Elizabeth's burial was attended strictly by members of her order, but a mass was held for her in Houston two days later at the church associated with the orphanage where she'd worked for so long.

Our Lady of Mercy Church was nearly full. Sister Mary Elizabeth had helped raise a lot of children, and most of those children had come, as adults, to do her this one last honor. Many of them were staying after the mass for what would be part wake, part reunion, in the church's rec center.

Jacy had flatly refused to consider staying, which hadn't surprised Tom at all.

He'd watched her. For the past two days, he'd watched her pull into herself. He'd seen the terrible shattering of grief streak across her face when he gave her the news, and he'd seen the terror in her eyes when she pushed him away.

She'd been retreating ever since.

The last two nights she'd slept in her bed, not his. She barely spoke to him during the days. Now, as the church emptied and people stopped to speak with her briefly, to hug or reminisce, he saw the same distance in her eyes when she spoke to people she'd grown up with that he saw when he looked at him.

It would be easier to keep hoping if he knew he was the only one she needed to retreat from.

So he was as prepared as a man could be when they got in the Jeep and she spoke without looking at him. "I'd like you to move out."

He twisted the ignition key. "We don't always get what we want, now, do we?" It took all his concentration to pull out into traffic at a reasonable speed instead of tramping on the accelerator.

"I know it would be inconvenient. If…if we don't stay together, everything will get pretty complicated, but—"

"Where do you suggest I go? Should I move into the storage unit with my couch? Dammit, Jacy, my name is on that lease next to yours."

"I need time! Just a little time to get myself together."

"Time?" Out of the corner of his eye he saw her hands twisting in her lap. That outward show of agitation gave him a certain savage satisfaction. "At least be honest. What you really want is for me to disappear. I'm too troubling to have around, aren't I?"

"Don't tell me what I want! You're always poking, prodding, trying to get me to respond—"

"You've responded pretty damned easily, too."

She shot him a dirty look. "I'm not talking about what happens between us in bed, though you've done your best to use that against me, too—withholding sex in an effort to get me to agree to marry you."

"What?"

"Do you deny that's what you were doing until…until you were hurt Monday? Trying to use sex to get me to agree—"

He cursed, briefly and fluently. "Trust. That's what it all

comes down to with us, doesn't it? I violated your trust once, and once is all anyone gets with you.'' He had a white-knuckled grip on the steering wheel. He took a deep breath and forced himself to relax slightly. "I kept my hands off you for a couple days, Jacy, because you had made it so damned obvious you didn't trust me. Even before we went to bed, you didn't really trust me. You'd never told me about Sister Mary Elizabeth. It hurt.''

She was silent a long time. Finally, as they turned onto Oak, she said softly, "I'm sorry. At one point I would have relished being able to hurt you. But I don't want to do that, not anymore. I just…I need some time to sort things out.''

"And you think you can do your sorting better if I'm not around.'' He was bitter.

"You're part of everything that's happened. Good Lord, Tom, in the last three months I've gotten pregnant and gotten dumped—''

"We're back to that again, aren't we?''

"I can't help it.'' She shoved her hair back. Her hand shook. He noticed, and a pang of alarm shot through the anger. "You seem to think I should be able to just set that aside, and I can't. But that's only part of everything that's happened to me. I nearly lost my baby. I had to leave my job. You moved in. I learned my mother's name, and that she's dead and my grandfather is in prison.'' She shook her head, unable to go on.

"And then Sister Mary Elizabeth died.'' He sighed and signaled his turn. "You've had a rough time of it, sweetheart, but I can help, if you'll let me.''

She glanced at him, her eyes big and hurting. "But you almost died, too.''

"Is that what this is about? My job?''

"I thought I could handle it,'' she whispered, looking away again. "And I could. I did, until…''

Until the woman who had raised you died, Tom finished silently for her. Until she knew from the inside out how much it hurt to lose someone to death. Tom understood. He *did*. He still wanted to grab her and shake some sense into her—to grab her and hold on tight, so tight she would never get away.

But she looked…fragile.

He'd seen Jacy furious, and he'd seen her fearful. He'd seen her passionate, needy, laughing and in pain…but he had never seen her look fragile before.

"All right," he said quietly as he turned into the apartment parking lot and pulled up beside her Mustang. "I'll bunk on my brother's couch for a while. But I'm going to come by every day to check on you, Jacy."

Jacy lay alone in the dark that night. It was what she'd wanted, what she'd insisted on, and it was terrible. She wanted to get up and peer in the closet. Look under the bed. Go back downstairs and check all the locks…again.

Only, of course, the monsters she feared were all right there with her.

She kept worrying about Tom. It was making her crazy.

Jacy felt as if she were dangling over a precipice, hanging on by her fingernails. She should have been sleeping, or at least struggling to understand the fear that had swallowed her whole the moment she heard of Sister Mary Elizabeth's death, but all she could think about was that she'd hurt Tom.

She couldn't stand that. But she couldn't forgive him, either. The hard knot of her own hurt wouldn't relax, wouldn't relent, wouldn't let her be around him while the fear was so strong. Yet she missed him. She'd lived on her own since she was eighteen, yet after only one month she missed Tom desperately.

That only made the fear worse. If she felt this bad after such a short time with him, how would she feel if she lost him after they'd been together a year or two?

She was strung impossibly tight between two choices she

didn't know how to make. Somehow she was going to have to, though. Somehow she would have to either let go of the hurt that wouldn't let her forgive, or let go of Tom.

Money can be reassuringly concrete. Jacy spent hours the day after Tom left trying to devise a way she could manage to live without him financially. If she couldn't come up with any answers that pleased her, she at least knew how to define the problem.

Nothing else in her life seemed equally tidy and subject to definition.

Tom called that afternoon when she was typing up her notes from an interview with a woman who'd given up her child for adoption twenty years ago.

"Jacy," he said as soon as she picked up the phone, "are you the 'anonymous source close to the police department' who tipped the *Sentinel* to the academy record of the rookie who shot me?"

She considered a number of responses, and settled for the simplest. "Yes."

He sighed. "I've been in the commissioner's office this morning, explaining that I'm not really in bed with the press just because I'm living with a journalist."

But they weren't living together, were they? Not now. And wasn't this a good example of how impossible the whole relationship was? "I'm sorry. I should have let you know so you'd be prepared for any fallout. But...it was the day before I learned about Sister Mary Elizabeth. I forgot."

He was silent a moment. "Understandable. But next time let me know, okay?"

"How much trouble are you in?" she asked worriedly. "I didn't get the information from you, after all. Surely you told them that." She'd checked out the rookie's police academy record herself, and passed on the information— which didn't make the department's hiring practices look too good, since he'd been taken on in spite of a record of reprimands involving repeated poor judgment.

"It's nothing I can't handle," he said dismissively. "Listen, why don't I bring some chow mein when I stop by tonight?"

"I don't think—"

"You don't have to eat it with me," he said brusquely. "But I will be by to check on you." He hung up without waiting on an answer.

That night he brought her chow mein and left without saying more than a few words. Her fortune cookie said she should expect good news soon from a distant place. She threw it away.

That night she turned on her radio so she wouldn't lie awake straining to hear the monsters. It was set to an oldies' station.

She expected to fret about Tom again, and about the choice she couldn't bring herself to make. But the radio played a song by the Platters, then one by the Supremes, and Jacy's mind drifted back to the past...to her life at the orphanage, and Sister Mary Elizabeth.

There were a lot of good memories, and they soothed her at first. But inevitably her thoughts led her to the biggest turning point of her life at St. Mary's—the day she'd accepted that her mother was never coming for her.

She'd turned seven years old that day. She'd had a party, of course—there wasn't much money, but there was always enough for cake and ice cream and a couple of modest presents when one of the girls had a birthday.

Later that afternoon Sister Mary Elizabeth had gone to tell one of the older girls, Katarina, that the court was sending her back to live with her mother again. Jacy had seen tears in the sister's eyes, and had naively supposed she was simply sad about Katarina leaving.

In the lonely darkness of Jacy's room, Simon and Garfunkel sang about being a rock...an island.

Jacy had been a little envious of the other girl's fortune. Katarina hadn't been happy about the court's decision. Nor had she thought much of Jacy's childish envy. "Get real," the girl had told her. "You're better off here than with your mom. She dumped you, right? Well, take it from me—it ain't no fun at all living with a stupid bitch who only wants you around when you've been gone long enough for her to forget how much trouble you really are."

Even then Jacy had known Katarina was speaking of her own experience, that not all mothers were like that. But she'd still spoken the truth. Real mothers—the kind a kid would want to claim—didn't dump their babies off on other people when they were too much trouble.

Suddenly she'd understood that the woman who had given birth to her hadn't been a real mother. Not someone she could count on—not someone she could *trust*. Yet the courts could decide to give Jacy to that woman, should she ever change her mind the way Katarina's mother had...and Sister Mary Elizabeth wouldn't be able to stop them. Just like she hadn't been able to make the court let Katarina stay there with them.

So Jacy had given up her fantasies about her mother on the same day she'd realized she couldn't think of Sister Mary Elizabeth as a mother, either. And she hadn't, though she had loved the sister dearly. Only tonight—tonight she could hardly breathe for the grief choking her.

The voice on the radio sang about rocks feeling no pain.

Islands never cry.

A single tear slipped down her cheek.

The next day she conducted a phone interview with a woman who had found her father after a ten-year search. The man hadn't been happy to meet his long-lost daughter. His wife—the same woman he'd been married to when he'd sired an illegitimate daughter—was furious when that grown daughter had initiated contact, throwing her family into turmoil.

But the man had two other children. After some of the dust had settled, one of them had decided she wanted a sister.

Exhausted, Jacy took a two-hour nap after that, waking up when Nan came over with take-out chicken. She stayed to eat the potato salad and explain to Jacy precisely why she was an idiot to let a man like Tom go.

For some obscure reason, Nan's nagging comforted Jacy. Maybe because it obscured how badly she missed Tom.

Then Tom showed up.

He let himself in with his key. As soon as Nan saw him she jumped up from the couch. "Oh, my goodness, look at the time! I've got to run."

He smiled. "Don't bother."

"No, really—"

"Really," he said firmly as he crossed to where Jacy sat, silent and trying to smile. "I'm not staying." He put one hand on the arm of the chair, bent and brushed a kiss across Jacy's surprised mouth. "How have you been?"

Was this the man she'd been worrying about having hurt personally, or damaged professionally? This calm, confident man who looked as if he'd slept beautifully the past two nights that she'd lain awake? "I'm fine," she said warily.

"Good." He straightened, reaching into his jacket pocket. "I see you've got company, so I won't stay."

Nan tried again. "I was just—"

"Leaving. I know. So am I." He held out a slip of paper, his eyes meeting Jacy's. "This is the name and phone number of a private detective in San Diego. He talked with your grandfather a few days ago, and has followed up on what Mulhoney told him. Call him if you want to, or let it go. The choice is yours."

He smiled at Nan then and offered to walk her to her car, but of course she wasn't going to leave now—not when she had something new to badger Jacy about.

Jacy didn't intend to call. What could Eagan Mulhoney say that had any bearing on her messed-up life? The search for her mother, for the identity of the person who had named her—what good had any of it done? She put the piece of paper in a drawer and told herself to forget about it.

At noon the next day she took it out and called. The line was busy. She hung up quickly, and couldn't understand why her heart was pounding so hard. As if she were excited, or very frightened.

She didn't try calling back.

That night, Tom came to see her again.

She was in the kitchen rinsing the steamer she'd used to fix vegetables for supper when she heard his key in the lock, and the door opening. "Jacy?"

Her heart lifted at the sound of his voice. She wanted to see him. She dreaded seeing him. "I'm in here." She dried her hands.

He came into the kitchen, smiling like he had the night before. Like everything was just fine in his life. He still had his hat on, and that blasted hat always did something to his features that made them impossible to read. But something about the way he moved as he walked toward her seemed less than certain.

He was carrying a large basket. It had a hinged lid, like a picnic basket.

"How are you feeling today?" he asked, setting his hat on the table.

The way he kept asking that question, as if she were suffering some illness, made her grouchy. "I feel lousy. Listen, if you brought supper I appreciate it, but I've already eaten."

That made his mouth quirk up. "It certainly isn't supper.

It's..." He stopped, ran one hand over his hair. *Definitely uncertain,* she thought, beginning to be intrigued.

"It's probably a dumb idea," he said, putting the basket on the counter between them. "But it occurred to me I've never given you any presents. I wanted to get you something."

Something that went in a picnic basket? "It's for me?"

Now he smiled with his eyes as well as his mouth. "Yes, it's for you. I can take it back if you don't like it."

She bit her lip, unaccountably shy, then reached out, opened the lid and peered in.

And got her nose licked.

She jerked back and stared as a wiggly little body covered in white, black and brown fur tried to climb out of the basket. "It's a puppy! It's a puppy, Tom!"

"Well, yes."

"You got me a puppy." She stared, frozen, for another second, then scooped it up before it had quite freed itself of the basket.

The puppy had dangly ears and a madly wagging tail and a warm, chubby tummy, and it wiggled all over with delight when she held it close. It tried frantically to lick her face. "It likes me," she said, amazed.

"Of course he likes you," Tom said wryly. "He's male."

She looked at Tom. Her eyes were giving her trouble, trying to tear up, and she repeated, "You got me a puppy."

"It was probably a dumb idea, but you wanted one when you were little. I thought—well, Sister Mary Elizabeth would have let you keep that puppy you found if she could have, so this is kind of from her, too."

She blinked hard, trying not to cry.

"Listen, I can take him back if you think he'll be too much trouble."

"No." She shook her head quickly. "Oh, no. This is—it's the best present anyone ever gave me, Tom."

He smiled slowly. "Good. That's good. Well," he said, "I'd better be going. There's some puppy food and stuff like that in a sack in the hall." And he turned around.

He was leaving? He'd walked in, blown away all her defenses, gotten her mushy and vulnerable, and he was leaving? "Tom?"

He looked at her and gave her that smile again, the one he'd given her when they made love the last time. "It will be all right, Jacy," he told her as he had once before, as if he really knew—which, of course, he couldn't.

And he left.

Jacy took the puppy outside and played with it until it—*he*—puddled on the patio. She brought him back in the kitchen and fed him, and read part of the book on puppy care that Tom had brought her and ended up taking the puppy outside again a little too late, but she didn't mind the cleanup. Then she sat in the living room because she couldn't bear to go upstairs and be alone, and the puppy fell asleep in her lap.

She kept petting him. The puppy didn't seem to mind.

Tom had given her the most thoughtful gift anyone had ever given her, then he'd left. If he really wanted her, why hadn't he stayed? She'd been desperately vulnerable to him, and he must have known it. He could have been back in her bed tonight, back in her life, if he'd pushed. And Tom didn't mind pushing to get what he wanted.

Why had he left?

She sat there, numb and bewildered, and stared at the shiny darkness caught in the glass of the patio doors. *Really,* she thought, *I ought to get up and pull the drapes closed.* But the puppy was sleeping so peacefully....

When she felt the first little poke in her stomach she thought the puppy had woken up. She looked **down,** but he slept on, unmoving.

Then it happened again—a funny, jiggly feeling. From the *inside.*

She sucked in her breath. Her hand went to her belly. She waited…and her baby moved again, and she felt it.

"Tom," she whispered. And she sat there treasuring the gifts he'd given her—one tonight, and one four months ago—and knew that even if he didn't come back, even if she barred him from her life forever or if he got tired of waiting for her to sort herself out and didn't want to come back, she wouldn't be completely alone. Because of what he'd given her.

That's when she started to cry.

She called the detective the next morning at ten o'clock, which, with the time difference, meant she caught him just as he was opening his office.

Samuel Evans was either expecting her call, or he was very organized. After the briefest exchange of civilities, he said, "Eagan Mulhoney gave me information about the man he believes to be your father, Ms. James, and my own investigation, coupled with that of Lieutenant Rasmussin, serves to confirm this. Do you want me to tell you what I've learned?"

She breathed slow and easy and petted the puppy in her lap and told Sam Evans she wanted to know everything.

"Your father's name is Dabir Ibn Kasib Abu Ahmed. He's a Saudi national who, with his family, was in this country illegally when he met your mother at a community college in an English as a second language course. He was seventeen when they met—a year younger than she was at the time. Because of his status as an illegal alien, they couldn't legally marry, although according to her father she considered them married 'in the eyes of God.' Mulhoney was worried about his daughter getting so serious so young, particularly with someone who was not of their faith, and tried to forbid the association. That's when they moved in together. They had lived together for nearly a year when she became pregnant."

He paused. "Dabir Ibn Kasib took you home from the hospital after your mother died from complications ensuing from childbirth. He moved back in with his family so that his mother could care for you while he worked, but the Immigration people caught up with them soon after that. He knew very little of American law, and was uncertain about whether you were a citizen or not—but he wanted you to stay here. He was worried for your safety. I believe his family had made some unwise choices, politically speaking, back in his home country. So before he was deported he managed to leave you at St. Mary's."

"On the steps of the orphanage," she said, her heart pounding steadily in her chest, her face wet with tears. "In a basket, with a note pinned to the blanket saying that my name was Jacinta Caitlin."

"Apparently he'd learned English mostly from books before coming to the States," he said. "He got some of his ideas of how life worked here from some old Gothic novels a missionary had left in his village many years ago. He was...very young, Ms. James."

Painfully young, she thought, swallowing. "How do you know so much?" she asked him. "How could your investigation uncover all this personal information?"

He hesitated again. "Your father wasn't difficult to trace, once I had his full name and the date of his deportation, which Lieutenant Rasmussin was able to obtain. I tracked him to a midsize town in the desert where he's lived ever since his return. Then, three days ago, I spoke with Dabir Ibn Kasib on the telephone. He filled in the gaps in the story I'd put together, and...he is eager to have contact with you, Ms. James. He never initiated contact himself because, for various reasons, he thought that was best for you."

"Mr. Evans?" she said when she could speak clearly. "Did he say anything about my name? How I got it?"

"I'm afraid not. Do you want me to contact him again?"

She thought for a moment. "No," she said at last. "Not

yet. Perhaps…perhaps I will ask him myself. Thank you, Mr. Evans.''

The puppy woke up when Jacy set the phone down. She put him on the floor before he could hurt himself falling off her lap, and he attacked her shoes happily, playing tug-of-war with the shoelaces and growling ferociously while Jacy sat and let the tears dry on her face.

Sister Mary Elizabeth had said that Jacy needed to learn about forgiveness, but there had never been anything to forgive, had there? There had been fear and love and loss, pain and confusion—for all of them. Because they were all just *people*. That's what it all came down to. People hurt and loved and lived and sometimes died, and mostly they did the very best they knew how to do. Mostly they never knew if what they did was for the best or the worst.

Like Tom…and her.

There was no one to blame, or to forgive.

Maybe that was the lesson.

An hour later, Jacy had showered and washed her face. She was brushing her teeth when the doorbell rang. And rang. And rang. Someone leaned on the buzzer several times before she got down the stairs.

Her heart gave one frightened leap when she glimpsed Raz through the peephole, but as soon as she opened the door she realized he wasn't all careful and blank the way he'd been when Tom was shot.

He was mad.

''I can't believe you'd do this to him,'' he said, coming in without waiting for an invitation.

She frowned and told herself to be patient. Naturally, Raz wouldn't be happy with her right now. Though it was odd that he'd had his brother sleeping on his couch for three days before he got upset enough to come chew her out. ''I know you're concerned about Tom, but you have to let us work things out ourselves.''

"Work things out?" He snorted in disgust. "Is that what you call it? Lord, Jacy, I thought you were different. Allison gave him enough grief about his job, but even she never asked him to quit."

"What are you talking about?"

"I'm talking about the fact that my brother is in his office right now, typing up his resignation. He's planning to leave the force so *you* won't have to worry about him."

Tom? Leave the police force? "That's *wrong,*" she said, appalled. "Tom is a cop. It's not just what he does. It's what he *is.*"

Raz eyed her sourly. "Well, if you've come to your senses, you'd better see if you can't get him to come to his. He's got an appointment with his boss in about fifteen minutes."

Twelve

Jacy called Tabor on her cellular as she pulled out of the apartment parking lot. She told him she needed him to keep Captain Edwards, Tom's boss, tied up for at least half an hour. Tabor, bless him, didn't ask questions—though she knew he would later. He promised to come up with something, and hung up.

It took her twenty-five of those minutes to reach "Cop Central."

She hadn't been here since the day she'd come to tell Tom he was going to be a father. The sergeant at the front desk was the same one who had been there last time—not such a great coincidence, since she was here during the same shift.

But this visit was different. This time he greeted her by name and commented on the chili dogs he'd eaten at her moving party. He asked if she was there on personal or professional business, and when she said personal, he handed her a visitor's badge without calling for Tom's approval.

As the elevator carried her slowly to the fourth floor she comforted herself with the idea that some things had changed a lot since the other time she'd been to Tom's office.

Not everything was supposed to change. Jacy didn't knock at his door this time, either, when she reached it.

Tom was working at his computer when Jacy opened the door. The blinds were partly open, and bright noon sunshine landed in hot bars on the dull gray carpet. The sleeves of his white shirt were turned up, and he looked as black-and-white as his office.

But she knew now there were colors inside this man—colors so rich and dripping with feeling they were shy of the very light they needed to bring them to life. And she knew that, in one sense, she'd been the one trapped in a black-and-white world, looking for perfect people to love in an imperfect world.

He turned his head. "Jacy?" He frowned. "Is something wrong?"

"I don't know," she said, and managed to get the door closed behind her. "Raz—Raz said—"

Tom's frown deepened. "What's he up to now?"

The family photos still lined the credenza behind him, but the big photo on the corner of his desk was gone. All at once Jacy was sure…of a great many things. "I think," she said distinctly, "that I've been had." Raz was, after all, an undercover cop. And undercover cops were nothing if not good actors. "Tom, were you planning on doing anything drastic today, like, for example, quitting the force?"

He cursed quietly and imaginatively. "I told my interfering idiot of a brother I was considering a leave of absence," he admitted. "That's all. If you were too upset by Sister Mary Elizabeth's death to handle my job right now,

I could take leave for a while. I never said anything about quitting.''

"Good," she said. Her blood had turned into champagne, fizzing dizzily in her veins. "That's good, because I wouldn't want you to."

He frowned at her, fierce and uncertain. "I'd do almost anything to make things easier for you, Jacy, but I'm a cop. I don't think I could change that."

"I know," she said, smiling at him tenderly.

He went still. "Do you?" Then he stood and came around his desk, stopping a few feet away. "What else do you know?"

Her heart began to pound. The quick clutch of nerves mixed with the fizziness in her blood. Her stomach lurched. "I know I...I want you to let your brother have his couch back. I want you to come home."

"I want that, too," he said softly. "But I need to be sure of something, Jacy. I need to be sure you know how I feel about you."

She waited, scared and delighted, for him to say the words—words she'd thought she'd never hear from this man, but was beginning to believe in, even unspoken.

"How do I feel, Jacy?"

She blinked. "Excuse me? Aren't you doing this backward?"

He smiled faintly. "I've done everything else wrong with you. Why should this be different?" His slight smile straightened. "I've told you how I feel in every way but words, Jacy. I need to know that you believe me. That you trust me. So...tell me how I feel."

Jacy had seen how Tom felt in his smile. She'd felt it in his touch, and been moved to tears by it when the puppy he gave her fell asleep in her lap while his child moved inside her. She *knew,* yet...

When she opened her mouth, fear trapped her, holding her in place as she dangled silently over the precipice where she'd hung for days. She licked her lips and breathed and reached inside, to the place that had been empty so long. And that's where she found the words. "You love me," she whispered.

His eyes closed. Then they opened, blazing—and he whooped and took two huge strides and grabbed her waist. "Thank God," he said, and he whirled her around. She laughed and held on to his shoulders while the world spun around them both. And then her feet touched the ground and his mouth came down on hers, and everything settled into place.

Tom kissed her the way a boy kisses his first girl, with hope and happiness, the fingers of one hand stroking her face tenderly. But his tongue was a naughty and clever rogue, not an innocent lad. It stroked along hers with all the knowledge and passion of the nights they'd spent learning each other.

Jacy kissed Tom back with the hope and innocence that had been hidden away in the empty place in her heart...and she ran her hand up his thigh with all the wicked intentions of any Eve for her Adam.

"Whoa," he said, stopping her hand just short of its goal. His lips were so close to hers, she felt his words as well as heard them. "I'm on a short fuse at the moment, sweetheart, and this isn't the right place."

She leaned forward half an inch and licked his lips. "Don't you have a lock on that door?"

He groaned. "Jacy, we are not going to make love in my office. The desk is too hard and the chairs are too small."

"There's always the floor." She ran her hand up his chest, smiling. "That sunny spot by the window looks pretty inviting."

"Not the floor, either." He pulled her against him, and now he said the words her heart had hungered for so long, spoke them clear and soft. "I love you, Jacy."

She rubbed her cheek against the crisp cotton of his shirt to praise him for saying it. "Me, too."

"Is that all I get?" he asked. "Just a 'me, too'?"

"I'm not sure if I've ever said it to someone," she told him. "I suppose when I was small...but I don't remember ever saying it, just straight out."

"It's not that bad. Try it."

She took a deep breath. "I love you." He was right—it wasn't bad at all. In fact, saying those words made her so happy it was a wonder she didn't float right off the floor. She leaned back, took his face in her hands and said it again, looking right at him this time—and grinning like an idiot. "I love you."

Of course he kissed her. Once they were both able to speak again, Tom said, "I fought what I felt for a long time. But the night when you let me make love to you again, though you had every reason not to...that's when I realized how much I needed you. I knew I'd been fooling myself. I don't know what I ever did to deserve a woman like you, but—"

"Wait a minute." She raised her head. "You've said that before. What do you mean, 'a woman like me'?"

His eyebrows lifted in faint surprise. "A beautiful woman," he answered simply. "A woman who could have any man she wanted."

Tears made Jacy's vision blur and sparkle. "Hormones," she explained with a sniff. "They make a woman weepy at times like this."

He smiled and dragged his thumb under first one eye, then the other. "I thought you said hormones had another effect on you. I'm afraid the door doesn't have a lock on it," he said as one hand wandered lazily around her body. "And I don't think a chair under the doorknob—"

The phone buzzed. Tom turned his head to scowl at it, and it buzzed again. "It's in-house," he muttered. "They can wait."

Reluctantly she pulled back as much as his arms would let her. "You'd better get it."

"Yeah." He sighed and let go of her. The desk was only one step away. He picked up the receiver. "Rasmussin." He listened, his grim expression giving way after a moment to a low chuckle. "Tell him you followed orders perfectly, and that she's standing real still at the moment." He hung up.

"That," he said, gathering her loosely in his arms again, "was my boss, who had an interesting talk with your boss forty minutes ago about some instructions you'd given him."

Instructions? Oh, good grief. She'd forgotten about calling Tabor on the way over here.

"Tabor told the captain he wasn't supposed to contact me, or allow me to contact him, for at least thirty minutes. He said he didn't know what was up, but he assumed it had to do with the chase you've been leading me on. They both hoped it meant you'd decided to put me out of my misery by standing still long enough for me to catch you."

She laughed. "Is that all I had to do? Stand still?"

Amusement faded from his eyes, leaving them as clear and cutting as the honor that was so much a part of him. "No, that's not all. I was pretty sure I had a chance with you once I realized *why* you asked me to move out. If you hadn't cared, you wouldn't have been so frightened. And since you're one of the bravest people I know, I figured you'd probably get past the fear, sooner or later. But it took more than courage to come here today. Have you truly forgiven me, Jacy?"

"It wasn't that hard to forgive you," she said quietly, "once I could forgive myself. You see, deep down I always thought I started out as someone's mistake. I felt like I'd made something good out of myself since then, but when you start out as a mistake, you try extra hard not to make any mistakes yourself."

"Jacy—"

"No, let me finish. I didn't really know I was doing that to myself. I just knew the world was a big, scary place, and I couldn't afford to make mistakes—the way I thought I'd done by going to bed with you the first time. Then I found out I was pregnant. I *couldn't* think of my baby as a mistake. But I was hurting so bad, it seemed like I had to have done something wrong. I thought the way I'd felt for you must have been the mistake."

She stopped to stroke his cheek. "Only you refused to act like the sorry SOB I wanted you to be. You kept behaving as if you were the man I'd fallen in love with. An honorable man. One who'd made a mistake—a wrong choice, like Sister Mary Elizabeth said—but who still deserved everything I had to give."

"Not 'deserve,'" he said gruffly. "Need. I do need you, Jacy."

Naturally she had to let him know how much his words pleased her, and it seemed best to make her point with her mouth...wordlessly. Somehow in the process she forgot the other things she'd meant to say—things about how easy trust turned out to be, because it was *Tom* to whom she'd given her heart and her trust.

He was a man who had fought to remain true to his first wife for three years after she died. Jacy didn't doubt that she would receive the same loyalty—a commitment that was just a little bit stronger than death.

"Tom," she said after several luxuriously distracting moments passed.

"Mmm," he said, and captured her mouth again so he could make persuasive comments with his tongue.

She almost forgot what she had to say. Almost. "Tom," she began again, pressing both hands to his chest to create enough distance to look him in the eye. "There is one more thing we need to talk about."

His breath came as unsteadily as hers, and his eyes

gleamed with obvious male intent. "You want to try propping the chair under the doorknob?"

She grinned. "Well, yes, but—no, wait a minute." She paused to clear her throat. "Are you going to marry me, or not?"

He grinned like the wolf he was, a wolf who had finally run down his prey. "I thought you'd never ask."

Epilogue

Four months & three weeks later

"**I** can walk." Jacy reached for the handle of the door, then froze as another contraction hit.

"Humor me." Tom opened the hospital door, waited and counted with her while the pain crested then ebbed. Then he scooped her up. "You're three weeks early."

"I know that. What time is it?" she asked as she grabbed his neck and held on for a quick, bumpy ride through the hospital doors.

"Four-ten," Tom said, but he didn't slow to look at his watch as he hurried toward Admitting. They'd come in last week to take care of the preregistration paperwork— *Just last week,* he thought, feverish with anxiety and anticipation. He hadn't even painted the nursery yet, and the wedding—

"We've got time, then," she said. "The contractions are

still seven minutes apart and the plane should have landed by now. Tabor is going to let Nan and your parents know, and you called Father Duchesne—you did call him, didn't you?''

"I had to leave a message," Tom said. Nurses were descending on them, one with a wheelchair. "He wasn't expecting to marry us for another two days, but you got in a hurry."

"Not me. I—" She embarrassed herself by clutching at him as he lowered her into the wheelchair. "I'm fine," she said, and made her hands let go.

"Jacy," he said, his eyebrows pulling together anxiously.

"Go on and park the car." She forced a grin because she'd worried him, dammit. "Me and my hormones are going to get checked in, then we're off to the birthing room. Right, nurse?"

"That's right," the woman behind the wheelchair said.

The room Jacy was wheeled into was an LDRP—hospital jargon for a room where everything from labor and delivery to recovery and postpartum care took place. Jacy had checked out almost every hospital in the metropolitan area before agreeing with her doctor on this one.

Her birthing room looked more like a hotel suite than a hospital room. It smelled like potpourri, not antiseptic. The floral print of the love seat and easy chairs mixed green and yellow with the soft blue of the walls, and on the table between the chairs sat a ceramic lamp much like the one Tom had once put his fist through. It was remarkably spacious for a hospital room.

Thirty-five minutes after the nurse helped Jacy into bed, the room was full of people and music. The music came from the CD player Tom had brought in from his Jeep along with Jacy's suitcase. The people came from Tom's family—and Jacy's.

While the Dixie Cups sang about going to the chapel to

get married, a white-haired man in the vestments and collar of a priest chatted with Jonathan Rasmussin, who kept darting uncomfortable glances at Jacy. She was making another circuit of the room on Tom's arm, looking lovely and extremely pregnant in a hospital gown covered by a long silk robe in peacock blue.

"Dammit, where are they?" Jonathan muttered.

Lydia, who'd been talking to Camille, overheard and laid a calming hand on her husband's arm. "They'll be here soon, I'm sure."

The door flew open and Nan hurried triumphantly into the room, trailing a yard of ribbons and lace from the frothy confection she held in one hand. "The veil!" she cried. "I just had to swing by the apartment on my way here and get this."

"One down and two to go," Tabor said, turning to Jacy. "You managed to pick the hospital farthest from the airport, didn't you?"

She scowled. "I wasn't planning on having my wedding here at the time."

No one commented on the fact that she could have gotten married months ago and not had to worry about the relative locations of hospitals and airports. They all knew why the wedding had been scheduled the way it had, and sympathized.

Even the increasingly impatient groom. "I'm going to kill that brother of mine if he doesn't get here soon."

"If he isn't here in—" Jacy began, then said, "Oh-oh." The contraction started small and built rapidly. She did her breathing the way she'd learned in Lamaze and squeezed Tom's hand and thought dark thoughts about the nurse who had told her she was still in the early, easy stages of labor.

It passed. Eventually.

"It's only been six minutes since the last one," Tom said grimly.

"If they don't get here in the next ten minutes," Jacy

said, "we'll go ahead without them." It wouldn't really matter, she told herself. Her wedding was not going to happen quite the way she'd planned it anyway, and she'd gone thirty-one years without—

Raz stuck his head in the door. "Is this where we're having the party?" Then he smiled and held the door open for the person behind him.

No one moved or spoke.

The man who stepped into the birthing room had the hawk nose and dark skin of a desert sheikh, though he was dressed more like the schoolteacher he actually was, in slacks and a light blue shirt. His hair was as black as his eyes, and his high cheekbones and wide mouth were older, more masculine versions of his daughter's.

His eyes searched the room, stopping on the very pregnant lady leaning on her groom's arm. "Jacinta?" he said uncertainly.

This time when Jacy's eyes teared up, she didn't try blaming it on hormones. She'd exchanged letters with this man, and learned she had three half-brothers and a half-sister on the other side of the world—and she'd learned, at last, where her name came from.

He and her mother had settled on "Caitlin" as her middle name, for Annabel's mother. But they'd been unable to agree on a first name, and after he brought her home, everyone in his family had wanted to name her something different. The one thing, he'd said, that everyone agreed on was that she was an unusually beautiful baby. So in the end he'd chosen the suggestion of another immigrant from yet another land. "Jacinta" meant "beautiful" in Greek.

When Dabir Ibn Kasib had agreed to set aside his pride enough to let Tom pay part of his plane fare so he could make the trip to the U.S., Jacy and Tom had put off their wedding to give him time to get the necessary papers. They'd talked on the phone several times since then. But

Jacy had never seen him—at least, not since she was two months old.

"Papa?" she whispered.

A smile broke over his face. Nerves, doubts and worry fell away as she laughed and cried and hugged her father for the first time.

Everything moved quickly after that. Father Duchesne herded them into their places, and before she knew it she was in bed again, holding Tom's hand while Lydia and Nan fastened the veil in place.

The hospital gown was old, the veil was new and her robe was certainly blue. Raz had the rings, Tom had the license and at the last minute Tabor added "something borrowed" by slipping his watch over her wrist, where it dangled like a bracelet.

"Dearly beloved," the priest said, while in the background Elvis sang, *"Love me tender, love me true…"*

When Jacy looked into Tom's eyes a few moments later and listened to the promises he made her, she believed with all her heart he would do just that.

Tom and Jacy Rasmussin
are thrilled to announce
the arrival of their daughter,
Annabel Elizabeth Rasmussin,
on February eleventh at 11:33 p.m.

* * * * *

Watch for Eileen Wilks's next sultry story—
THE VIRGIN AND THE OUTLAW coming May
1998 from Silhouette Intimate Moments.

Return to the Towers!

In March
New York Times bestselling author

NORA ROBERTS

brings us to the Calhouns' fabulous
Maine coast mansion and reveals the
tragic secrets hidden there for generations.

For all his degrees, Professor Max Quartermain has a
lot to learn about love—and luscious Lilah Calhoun is
just the woman to teach him. Ex-cop Holt Bradford is
as prickly as a thornbush—until Suzanna Calhoun's
special touch makes love blossom in his heart.
And all of them are caught in the race to solve
the generations-old mystery of a priceless
lost necklace…and a timeless love.

Lilah and Suzanna
THE
Calhoun Women

**A special 2-in-1 edition containing
FOR THE LOVE OF LILAH and
SUZANNA'S SURRENDER**

Available at your favorite retail outlet.

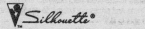

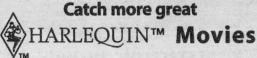

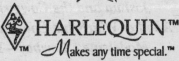

ALICIA SCOTT

Continues the
twelve-book series—
36 Hours—in March 1998
with Book Nine

PARTNERS IN CRIME

The storm was over, and Detective Jack Stryker finally had a prime suspect in Grand Springs' high-profile murder case. But beautiful Josie Reynolds wasn't about to admit to the crime— nor did Jack want her to. He believed in her innocence, and he teamed up with the alluring suspect to prove it. But was he playing it by the book—or merely blinded by love?

For Jack and Josie and *all* the residents of Grand Springs, Colorado, the storm-induced blackout was just the beginning of 36 Hours that changed *everything!* You won't want to miss a single book.

Available at your favorite retail outlet.

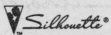